ABOUT THE AUTHOR

Penny Freedman has taught Latin, Greek, English, Drama and Linguistics in schools, colleges and universities in London, Kent and the West Midlands. She has also been a theatre critic and an amateur actor and director. Her earlier books, *This is a Dreadful Sentence, All the Daughters, One May Smile, Weep a While Longer, Drown My Books, Little Honour, Where Everything Seems Double, Chronicles of the Time,* and *The Scottish Play,* featuring Gina and Freda Gray and DCI David Scott, are all published by Troubador.

COME
TO
DUST

PENNY FREEDMAN

T

Troubador Publishing Ltd
Unit E2 Airfield Business Park,
Harrison Road, Market Harborough,
Leicestershire LE16 7UL
Tel: 0116 279 2299
Email: books@troubador.co.uk
Web: www.troubador.co.uk

ISBN 978-1-80514-540-0

British Library Cataloguing in Publication Data.
A catalogue record for this book is available from the British Library.

Printed and bound in Great Britain by 4edge Limited
Typeset in 11pt Palantino by Troubador Publishing Ltd, Leicester, UK

For the biochemists and microbiologists of my acquaintance
– if they can forgive me.

Apologies and Disclaimers

The idea of a murder at a scientific conference was suggested to me many years ago by an old friend, Alan Malcolm, a professor of biochemistry, and I am grateful to him, but I am also conscious of blundering into territory that I know only at one remove. So I have some pre-emptive apologies to make.

The academic disagreement about the comparative nutritional value of GM and non-GM crops is entirely my invention, and may, for all I know, be nonsense. And those who know what they really mean may be annoyed by my use of specific biochemical terms as chapter headings. Years ago, I was delighted to learn that there are proteins that go around assisting other proteins, and are named *chaperones*. This was my starting point, and I hope some people will enjoy the headings.

It is an important element of the plot of this book that a character has been diagnosed with Alzheimer's. I have several friends who are caring for partners with this devastating disease, and I apologise sincerely to them if they feel that I have been insensitive or cavalier in writing about it.

Finally, my thanks to my daughter, Genny, for expert information about insulin injections, acquired over the past twenty-five years.

Chapter One

FREE ENERGY

Saturday

'What exactly are you punishing yourself for?' she asked, and Detective Superintendent David Scott used all the breath he could muster to gasp, 'Sins of omission,' before closing his phone and shoving it into his pocket. As an answer it was hardly true, but it had the virtue of being short, and he certainly didn't have the breath to challenge the premisses of her question.

Why did he perform this weekly ritual – this bone-shaking jog along the Embankment in the early hours of every Saturday morning? He could have told Gina that it was for her benefit – that she wouldn't want him fat and flabby – and there was some truth in that. He could have pointed out that early morning was the only time to run, before the tourists were out and ambling. He could have lied outright and told her he enjoyed it. Or he could have admitted that it was a ritual from the years before he met her, the years when weekends were lonely deserts and being on duty was a lifesaver. But then he would have had to admit to being grateful to her for saving him from that, for sweeping him up into her whirl of activity. But you didn't show that kind of weakness to Gina – it could always be used as ammunition.

Met HQ was in sight, and his heart lifted – not just because he could stop running, but because he enjoyed going in like this, when the floors were still wet from their early morning cleaning, and the place was empty and silent, and he could read over anything that had come in overnight without interruption. And if he was scrupulously honest, he liked being the first to sign in – devotion to duty writ large.

He slowed his pace, and was starting to jog across the road when he heard a sound behind him, something between a yell and a scream. He turned to look, and saw a couple locked together, the man with his hands round the woman's throat, forcing her towards the river barrier. Pulling his warrant card out of his pocket, he ran back.

As he shouted, 'Police!', the man pushed the woman away from him violently and took off at a run. Scott forced his leaden legs into a sprint and caught up with him, grabbing him by the back of his T-shirt and getting hold of one arm. The man turned, writhing in his grasp, grabbing hold of Scott in his turn, and as Scott held on hard and started the routine words of an arrest, he felt the sudden sharp pressure as a knife slipped in between his ribs.

Chapter Two

REDUCTION

Saturday

There is no dignity, absolutely none, to be found in sitting on a plastic chair in a hospital corridor, waiting for news. Quiet composure is beyond us, we who sit here, oscillating between hope and resignation, nerve ends alert to the slightest signal, the merest inkling of what is going on behind the closed doors. People go in and come out of the doors, but they stride past us with the practised detachment that defies us to jump up and pester them with our questions. I say *our* because I am not alone here. Although it is not yet nine o'clock in the morning, several other people are sitting here, yanked abruptly from the routine rhythms of their Saturday morning, inappropriately dressed for terror and death.

It is a small triumph that I have got this far at all – that I am not still sitting with the remnants of the Friday night drunks in A&E. David's pretty protégée, DI Rula Bartosz, rang me with the incomprehensible news at seven-thirty this morning, and though I was shaking from shock and two espressos consumed on the run, I had the sense to announce myself as David's *partner* when I stormed up to the triage desk, unkempt and breathless. It is a term I usually shun as inadequate to describe our oddly conjoined yet divided relationship, but *keep it simple,* I told myself. *Don't alienate them.* I failed to convince, though. The triage nurse surveyed me through narrowed eyes. I guess you develop pretty good bullshit antennae in her job, and hers were telling her I was trouble.

'We can only give out information to next of kin,' she said. 'Are you Mr Scott's next of kin?'

'Well, I'm not kin, but he is the only child of long-dead parents,' I told her. 'So how does that work?'

'And you are…?'

'His closest kith.'

'Name?'

'Virginia Gray.'

'Address?'

Here, low cunning told me to give David's address, although it is in no sense my home, and I avoid going there because its beige neutrality screams, *for the man who lives here, his work is his life.*

And then she asked to see my driving licence, and I gaped at her in bewilderment.

'I don't drive. It wasn't a car accident,' I blurted. 'He was stabbed. I wasn't there. I had just been talking to him on the phone.'

She sighed. 'I need proof of address, if you claim you're his partner.'

I was about to burst into a furious diatribe about time-wasting and intrusion and everything that was wrong with the NHS, when Rula arrived and saved me. She was as unkempt as me, pale-faced and red-eyed, but she flashed her warrant card, demanded to know where David was, and got an immediate answer from my interrogator, who suddenly turned sweet as pie for her.

'Through the door there,' she said, ever so meekly. 'Dr Ghosh will talk to you.'

Rula took hold of my arm to lead me to the door indicated, but I wasn't going that easily. I turned back to the nurse.

'And he is not Mr Scott,' I hissed. 'He is Detective Superintendent Scott.'

'Oh, we know,' she said. 'We're prepared.'

'What did she mean?' I muttered to Rula as she marched me along.

She stopped and looked at me. 'It's top of the news, Gina. A senior police officer stabbed outside Met HQ. There are reporters outside already.'

Oh my God. I hadn't thought of the public dimension at all, but of course I could see it:

Top Met Cop Knifed

London Crime Out of Control

Is the Met Fit for Purpose?

'There'll be questions in Parliament,' I said.

'Bugger Parliament,' she said. 'I just want to catch the fucker who did this.'

So now she has gone, back to join the team that has been hastily assembled, detectives and uniforms, forensic officers and dog handlers, for all I know, summoned back from their weekend leave, and I am sitting here on my own, the plastic chair clammy under my thighs, waiting.

Rula did get some information before she left me, courtesy of Dr Ghosh, who looked far too young to know anything, and now I know that it is much worse than I had imagined – and my worst imaginings were pretty bad. All I knew was that David had been stabbed, and my terrors were of disastrous blood loss, damaged organs and shock, but it turns out that the stabbing is the least of it. There is a skull injury, a haemorrhage. David is in a coma.

'They think the fucker kicked him in the head,' Rula said. 'They've done a brain scan. Not good news. I'm going back

5

to work. Do you want to leave? There'll be no news here for a while.'

'What am I going to do if I'm not here?' I said.

So here I am.

I have stopped looking at my watch, so I have lost track of how long I have been here. The staff have continued to ignore me. I am trying very hard to keep my temper, but I resent being made to feel importunate. It doesn't suit me. My inclination is for a tantrum, and I am precariously close to it by the time a nurse emerges from one of the mystery doors and actually catches my eye. She comes over to me.

'You've been here for a while, haven't you?' she asks.

'David Scott ,' I say. 'I'm waiting for news.' Then I add, 'I'm his partner,' in the hope that I will sound more convincing this time.

Her immediate reaction is unmistakeable alarm.

'We didn't realise you were still here,' she says, and then she crouches down beside me, like cabin crew do when dealing with nervous fliers. They go on courses, I suppose, that tell them that you can be more empathetic if you don't stand over people. So she does all the right things – speaks softly, makes eye contact, takes hold of my hand – but the bottom line is that she is sending me home. David is in a coma, in the ICU, and can't be visited. There is no place for me here.

'You can phone in tomorrow,' she says, 'but we'll ring you if there's any change.'

I hear her knees crack as she pulls herself upright.

I get up and nearly grab hold of her. I can't let her go.

'But you can help people out of comas, can't you?' I say desperately. 'I could help. I can talk to him. He might respond to my voice.'

She pats me gently. 'That might be useful later,' she says. 'This is going to be a long business, I'm afraid, and he's not ready for that yet.'

And then she goes, back behind her magic door, and I wander blindly along corridors with signs advertising treatment for all the appalling things we might die of, until I stumble out into daylight, and find myself at the front of the hospital, where there are BBC and Channel Four vans, plus a crowd I take to be reporters, and I can't avoid the thought that they would actually quite like David to die, because it would make a better story.

I sidle past them, an unremarkable messy-looking woman in unmatched clothes, and I start to make for Westminster Underground, only to give up and flag down a taxi when the complexities of a tube journey seem altogether too much. In the taxi, I try to order my thoughts, to make a plan for a day that is not now going to include a haircut and a trip to the Globe with David, but my ability to plan seems to have gone along with everything else. I can't think beyond getting out of these clothes. After that, the most appealing option is crawling back into bed.

It turns out that even that is off the agenda. My flat, as we approach it, is unrecognisable. A scrum of people is blocking the pavement and even, it seems, occupying the steps down to my basement front door.

'Drive on past,' I shout to the driver.

'So where to?' he asks, as he does as he is told.

A good question. 'Just drive round the square,' I say, though I realise that we can do this only once before the news hounds are onto us. How have they found me? I am so unofficial that even if David has a Wikipedia entry – does he? I don't know – I won't be mentioned. For a moment I'm inclined to blame Rula for giving me away, but why would she? *A & E*, I think. *That bloody triage nurse, and me shouting that I am David Scott's partner before helpfully spelling out my name.*

Where to go? To Ellie in Kent? Annie in Scotland? Eve in Cumbria? All impossible because I can't leave London, can I?

'Drop me off here,' I call to my driver as my beleaguered flat comes into view for the second time. I get out and pay and watch him drive away, and just as I am thinking that my only option is to sit on the pavement and cry, a voice calls, 'Signora Gina,' and I look round to see Alessandro. Just along the road is Cucina Nonna, my local restaurant, and the proprietor is standing outside it with his arms open. I have enough sense to know that the arms are a gesture of welcome, and I am not supposed to fall into them, so I burst into tears instead.

Murmuring soothing Italian noises, he ushers me into the empty restaurant, and I realise that it is only just midday, although this day has been going on forever. He sits me down and brings me a glass of grappa and a slice of almond cake. 'For the sugar,' he says, and then sits down opposite me. 'We saw him – Signor David – they showed a picture on TV – *Breaking News*. And then those journalists.'

I take a tentative sip of the grappa. It might make me feel better, but it might make me throw up.

'How long have they been there?' I ask.

He shrugs. 'Two hours maybe.'

'I wonder how long they'll stay.'

'Your daughters will come,' he says. 'They will look after you.'

'They don't know.'

'You didn't phone them?'

'No. They're busy, and ...'

'They must know by now,' he says. 'They didn't call you?'

I rummage in my bag and find my phone, which has been switched off ever since I was taken into the inner sanctum at the hospital. I switch it on, and it immediately becomes hysterical, writhing, squawking and flashing its lights as messages come pouring in. I can see at a glance that several of them are from Ellie and Annie.

'Yes, they know,' I say.

'And you will go and stay with one of them,' he says firmly.

'Oh no, no, no. I have to be in London, and Ellie is busy with a new job, and—'

My phone rings. I look at it. The caller is the only person I can face talking to at this moment.

'Hello, Freda,' I say.

Chapter Three

HELIX

Saturday

Freda sat on her bed, looking at her phone. Mum had said not to ring Granny. Sending a text was OK, but she was probably at the hospital and ringing was intrusive. And yet. And yet she thought Granny would need to talk – she always needed to talk – and Freda needed to hear her. And Granny was no good at texts. They were always short and stilted and sometimes so full of typos they were incomprehensible. She punched the number and was answered almost immediately.

'Hello, Freda.'

'Are you all right, Granny?' she asked.

'Alessandro is looking after me with brandy and cake, so I'm better than I was ten minutes ago. There are people camped outside my flat. I don't understand how everyone knows.'

'It's all over social media, Granny,' she said. 'David, you, everything.' Then she took a breath. 'There's no real news about David, though – just horror stories. What's happened to him?'

She waited, and thought she heard the clink of a glass. Then her grandmother cleared her throat.

'He's in a coma,' she said. 'I wasn't allowed to see him.'

'Because of losing a lot of blood?'

'Blood?'

'The knife wound.'

'The knife wound is the least of it, my love. But I shouldn't say any more. The police may not want the details to get out.' She made a noise that almost sounded like a laugh. 'David would smile – me getting discreet, finally,' she said, but her voice broke on the last word, and she went on, 'I can't talk about this anymore. Tell me where I'm going to sleep if I can't get into my flat. I'm thinking of going in to my office and sleeping on the floor.'

'Go to our house,' Freda said. 'Mum will look after you, and you can sleep in my room. I'm not there.'

'Why? Where are you?'

'I've got a job.'

'A job? Is reintroducing child labour La Truss's latest bright idea?'

'I'm sixteen and I'm not going up chimneys,' Freda said.

'What are you doing?'

'Temporary domestic staff at Stour College. It's a conference.'

'And Mum is all right with you doing that?'

'Yes.' *Why wouldn't she be?* Freda wondered.

'She probably hasn't been to conferences. People go mad, Freda. They say, *What happens at conference stays at conference,* then they drink themselves stupid in the bar and jump into one another's beds.'

She was sounding a bit hysterical, Freda thought. 'This lot really don't look like that, Granny', she said. 'They're all old.'

'They're the worst. Lock your bedroom door. What's the conference on?'

'*Genetic Modification and Nutritional Advantage.* Faith says it's a fusion thing – ecology meets biochemistry, meets medicine.'

'A laugh a minute, then. So Faith's there too? She's the girl I saw playing Imogen in that open air *Cymbeline* we saw in the summer, isn't she?'

'Yes. She got me the job. Me and Lisa. Her stepdad is helping to organise it. He's a professor at Marlbury Uni. But seriously, Granny. Stay at our house. I won't be back till Monday night, and I'll sleep on the sofa.'

'I'll think about it, darling. It was good to talk to you.'

She was just about to ring off when Freda remembered what she had wanted to tell her.

'Granny,' she said, 'something spooky. There's someone at the conference who says she knows you. You taught her English, apparently.'

'I've got former students all over the place,' her grandmother said.

Freda could hear that she didn't really want to know about this, but a distraction would be a good thing, wouldn't it? So she went on.

'It was really weird. I was just finishing cleaning her room this morning – this was before we heard the news about – you know – when she came back from breakfast, and she looked at my name badge, and then she looked hard at my face, and she said, '*Yes it could be.*' Then she said she had met me when I was just a baby, and that you were a wonderful teacher and she owed you a lot. Actually, I think she said she owed you everything.'

'What's her name?'

'Her name badge says *Dr Irina Boklova*.'

There was a long pause, and she waited.

'Well, that's a stunner,' her grandmother said, and the phone went dead.

Chapter Four

CHAPERONE EFFECT

Saturday

When I stop talking to Freda, I realise that I have finished my grappa, and I am feeling woozy. Alessandro was right about the cake. I pick up my fork and start to eat it, and with the sugar rush come the beginnings of a plan, forming effortfully in the primordial soup that is, just for the moment, standing in for my brain. I don't want to go and stay with Ellie and sleep among the hopeful secrets of a teenage bedroom. They would be kind to me – Ellie, Ben and Nico – but kindness will undo me. Even Alessandro's solicitude has made me feel weak and weepy. What I want is a quiet hole to crawl into, and some time alone to think and feel. I expected that would be my flat, but the Fourth Estate has put paid to that, and I have realised that even the option of sleeping on my office floor is unavailable owing to new security measures at the college which make it impossible for us to go in at weekends without triggering alarms. What I need is an anonymous room in a quiet hotel, and where better than Stourly, home of Stour Agricultural College? I don't really think that Freda will be exposed to the unwanted attentions of lecherous academics, but it is possible. She is very pretty.

And if I can't do anything for David, I might at least be helpful to her.

Alessandro brings me a milky latte as I am finishing the cake. I drink it while googling places to stay in Stourly, and find The Mitre, a pub with rooms just across the road from the college. I am in a weak enough state to take this as a sign of divine providence, and I book it. Then I go to the loo.

My face, in the mirror above the basin, is a white horror with blazing cheeks and demented eyes, emerging from a tangle of Brillo pad hair. I find a comb and an ancient lipstick in my bag, apply them half-heartedly, and think about emergency purchases before I go for the train.

Alessandro refuses to let me pay for anything, as I knew he would. I assure him that I will go and stay with Ellie, and he ushers me out. The restaurant is filling up now, and I should think he is glad to be rid of me – a death's head if ever there was one. I set off for M&S, making a mental shopping list as I go.

It doesn't take me long to buy what I need, mainly because I can't bear to be here – I can't bear the normality of it, the cheerful Saturday bustle, the weekend beginning and the promise of leisure to come. I buy some black trousers and a black top. I don't mean to be funereal but to my eyes everything else looks horribly gaudy. I add underwear, socks, a slip of a nightdress, toothbrush and toothpaste, and rely on The Mitre to supply the rest. When I have paid, I find the loos and, in a tiny cubicle, I take off the saggy pull-ons and ancient T-shirt I found on a chair in my bedroom this morning, and wrestle myself into the new stuff. I did at least have the sense to put on some decent black boots this morning, and I grabbed a respectable jacket from a hook in the hall as I went out, so there is a chance that The Mitre will let me in. I cram my other purchases into my bag, find a bin to dump my discarded clothes in, and hail a taxi.

It is a forty-five minute train journey to Stourly. Not too far from London, I tell myself. If I am needed at the hospital, I can be back in no time, though I can't imagine how I can be needed, really. All the same, while I am waiting for the train I do ring the hospital. The kindly nurse said I could, didn't she? Except that, of course, I can't. When I say I am David Scott's partner, I am stonewalled: *Superintendent Scott's condition remains stable but critical.* I should have thought – every reporter in the capital will be claiming to be David's partner, sister, brother, son, daughter. How am I ever going to know anything? Frantic now, I find Rula's number, which she put in my phone before she left me at the hospital, and when she answers, I blurt, 'Is there any news?'

'We've only just started, Gina. Forensics have been at the scene, we've put out an appeal for witnesses and we're going through the responders, but it's not—'

'I don't mean the attacker. I mean David. I can't get anyone at the hospital to talk to me. *Stable but critical* is all I get. I thought they might have talked to you.'

I hear a release of air. It is a sigh that she is trying to stifle.

'*Stable but critical* is good,' she says. 'And I'm afraid they'll only contact us if there's a change that – you know – affects the nature of our investigation.'

'What do you mean?' And then I know. 'You mean if it becomes a murder case?'

'Look, Gina. No news is good news for the moment. They did the surgery and now we wait. I know it's hard. Have you got someone to be with?'

'I'm fine,' I lie. 'But you'll let me know if you hear anything?'

'Trust me.'

The train arrives and is quite empty. On this time-skewed day it is not yet rush hour – not even going home from school time. I sit in an empty carriage and craft careful text messages to Ellie and Annie. I can't phone because they will hear that I am on a train, but I take care with the messages, apologising for the delayed replies, blaming hospital rules about phones, passing on *stable but critical*, returning love, tactfully refusing offers of company and hospitality, promising to pass on any news. I despatch them and then text Freda:

Coming to stay at The Mitre. Will explain later.
DON'T TELL MUM
XX

The Mitre turns out to suit me perfectly: the staff are offhand, my room smells nasty, and there is no food being served this evening because the chef is off. There is no chance of my enjoying myself here; this is not a treat. I am hungry, though, and since I don't want to be wandering round later looking for somewhere to eat dinner on my own, I decide to go and find a café for a substantial tea. If I eat mainly cake today, so be it.

I find the café I had in mind. There was a time, when I was first teaching at Marlbury University, when I was detailed to come out here once a week to give English coaching to a student from Eritrea. He was here on a British Council scholarship, studying agricultural development of some sort, and under the terms of his scholarship he was entitled to one-to-one English teaching. So that was me, and I used to get the train out here on a Saturday morning and have coffee and a scone in here before going to do my hour with him. He was very bright and there was nothing the matter with his English, really, but he wrote an essay for me every week, and we went through it before he produced a list of questions he wanted to ask me about British culture, which puzzled and intrigued him. All I can say is, the more you try to explain British culture to someone who has not grown up with it, the more peculiar it seems. Anyway, the café is still here, and I sit down with a pot of tea and a tuna sandwich which makes me feel slightly sick, but I munch my way through it stoically all the same. I also text Freda to tell her that I am here.

After that, there is nothing for it but to go back to my room and, finally, to allow in the doubts and terrors that I have been keeping at bay all day. And what I know is that the fear of losing David is not as terrible as the fear of losing David as I know him, and having him replaced by a new David – impaired, diminished, inarticulate, angry. Could I look after him? I can't imagine it. Looking after one another is not something we do, he and I. I don't think I have ever so much as offered David an aspirin.

Unbidden, suddenly, a memory comes to me from what must be fifteen years ago. I am lying in bed at home after a night in hospital, my head bandaged after an attack with a piece of scaffolding, and David is there, standing at my bedroom window, looking out at the black November evening. Has he asked me how I am? I don't think so. What he is doing is talking to me about child pornography. Together we are piecing together a theory about a murder. Do I mind that he is not fussing over me? Not a bit. This conversation is much more interesting.

So, what I am contemplating is so alien I can't get hold of it. Instead, I find my brain skittering off to practicalities – to wheelchair access to my flat, to hoists and rails and a second bathroom, to disability-oriented computer programmes, to therapies and professional care.

I can't do this anymore. I need distraction. I am thinking that I may be forced to go downstairs to the gloomy bar when my phone trills. There is a message from Freda. She will be here soon.

Chapter Five

PEER REVIEW

Saturday

When they had cleared away the lunch, Faith and Lisa washed up while Freda put out everything that was needed for tea and coffee in the break in the afternoon conference session. It was self-service, from tables set up at the back of the lecture hall, but it was her job to put the urns on to heat at the right time and to be there in case of any problems.

By the time everything was out, people had started trickling into the hall, and she remembered that the programme stuck to the door showed that Granny's student, Dr Boklova, was giving a talk next. She would quite like to hear her, she thought, even if she didn't understand the science. Granny might want to know what her English was like, and it would be a good distraction for Granny if she could report back on the talk. If she just sat here quietly at the back, would anyone mind? There were glasses and a jug of water on the table, in case anyone needed a drink, so if she sat herself near those, she could look as though she was on duty.

Her instinct that she would be more or less invisible was confirmed when Dr Boklova came in and went straight to the front of the room, to where things were set up for her talk.

Others started to trickle in, and Freda was already beginning to recognise some of them. They were the ones who stood out from the majority, who were mostly male, boringly white, and drearily dressed.

There was the little American woman, who made a huge fuss about what she ate – which wasn't much – and was like a skinny little bird. It was hard to say how old she was – once people were old, you couldn't really tell – but Freda guessed she was at least seventy, but she had her white hair long, with an Alice band, like a little girl, which was weird, and she always had two or three young people with her, who were like her carers, carrying her papers, finding her the right seat, bringing her coffee, and chipping in with complaints about food and drink on her behalf. She was old but she didn't look disabled: she walked all right and she could obviously see, so why did she need all this attention? Freda had heard some of the older scientists call her *Susan*, but her minders called her *Dr Kessler*, so Freda thought they must be her students, though they looked a bit old for that. Maybe postgraduates, like the ones Granny taught. And maybe they were just toadying, hoping for good grades or whatever.

The other woman she had noticed stood out by not being white, and by announcing it by wearing a sari. She looked quite young, but Freda had heard her sounding quite forceful in a discussion at lunchtime, and she had one of those Indian accents that made her sound rather posh.

Among the men, there was Hywel Jones, Faith's stepfather, and Professor Peter Pratt, who seemed to be helping to run the conference. (If you had to lumber your child with the surname *Pratt*, did you have to make it worse by calling him *Peter*? And then, if you had to be Peter Pratt, wouldn't you want to go into a job where you didn't add *Professor* to that?) Apart from them, the only man she had noticed – and resolved to stay well away from – was a man called Kevin. He was probably

Dr Something, but she hadn't heard anyone call him anything other than *Kevin*. He was pretty old but he wore his shirt unbuttoned way too low, with a load of sad grey chest hair showing. His actual hair was darker, and she wondered if he dyed it. He obviously thought he was God's gift, and it was quite amusing to see how all the women avoided him. He had an annoying accent, too. Freda wasn't good at knowing the different types of northern accent, but whatever his was, it was so exaggerated she was sure he was putting it on.

She watched him now, as he came bouncing into the hall, looking for attention, and then she lost sight of him because something quite unexpected happened. Hywel Jones came bustling in, smiling and cheery as always, and coming in with him was a pretty, dark woman whom Freda had seen going around with Dr Boklova. The woman stopped at Freda's table to pour herself a glass of water, and Hywel Jones came round behind her, said something in her ear which Freda couldn't hear, and *stroked her bottom*. It was so unexpected that Freda felt her mouth drop open – only to drop further when the woman turned round and threw her glass of water in his face. He spluttered and tried to laugh it off, Freda jumped up and offered him a tea towel which was in place to catch drips from the tea urn, and the woman walked away and took a seat in the front row. Not many people seemed to have noticed what had happened because they were mostly looking towards the lectern at the front, but Dr Boklova had seen it definitely, and she looked furious. Furious with Hywel Jones or furious with her friend for making a scene? Freda couldn't tell.

She didn't understand much of Dr Boklova's talk. It was about GM food, and Freda was able to glean that her research had shown problems with it – something about nutritional advantage, she gathered that much, but that was about it. Still, she could report to Granny that Dr Boklova's English was good. It was very American, actually, which she wouldn't have got from Granny's teaching but had obviously got from California. Her accent reminded Freda of Martina Navratilova's quite a lot, but Dr Boklova had better hair.

The real fun started when it came to questions, and it was Hywel Jones who fired the starting gun. Dr Boklova had mentioned his research in her talk, and obviously disagreed with it, and he seemed to be furious – and probably having water thrown over him hadn't helped. He was very much being the big man, as though she had no right to disagree with him, and then others started chipping in, and it looked as though it was going to be a women versus men argument. Dr Parvati Varma jumped up to say that her research on GM foods in India supported Dr Boklova's findings, and Dr Susan Kessler said, in her quacky little old lady voice, that her group's findings were in agreement with Dr Boklova's. Professor Pratt, who was in charge of the meeting, invited Hywel Jones to say something about his research on the subject, but he had hardly started before Dr Parvati Varma was on her feet again, and Freda couldn't follow everything that she said, but she was talking about a paper being rejected for publication, and Hywel Jones was very red in the face by now and shouting about *referee confidentiality*, and Dr Varma turned to him and asked, 'Have those experiments that the referees recommended been done now?'

Everyone waited for an answer, looking at Hywel Jones, but he waved an arm at a weedy-looking young guy sitting near the back of the hall, and said, 'Well, Dr Crawley. This is your work. Have those experiments been done yet?'

The young man looked as though he wasn't going to answer, but stayed in his seat with his head bowed. Then he stood up, and Freda, who was close to him, could see that he was furious. Then he spoke, and he had one of those annoying public school drawls like some of the boys at Marlbury Abbey school had.

'It was my clear understanding from our discussions that the research was to go in a different direction, and that you did not consider it a justifiable use of resources to undertake those experiments. I was in disagreement, but you prevailed.'

And with that he walked out of the hall.

Then there was a weird silence with no-one looking at anyone else, until Kevin – the chest hair guy – laughed and said, 'Well, looks like that's it, folks,' and Professor Pratt said he thought it was probably teatime, and Freda was glad that she had switched the urn on as soon as Dr Boklova had finished giving her talk. He thanked Dr Boklova, and once everyone had clapped they all started talking and Hywel Jones walked out, looking furious.

Busy helping people with their tea – really, considering they were scientists, some of them were amazingly helpless at managing a tea urn – Freda was itching to get this stuff cleared up and go and see her grandmother. If anything could be a distraction from her worries, this just might be.

Chapter Six

GENETICALLY MODIFIED

Saturday

When there is a knock on my door I am so certain that it is Freda that I call out, 'Come in, darling,' and jump up to hug her, but the door doesn't open immediately, and when it does, it is not Freda's head that appears. A youngish woman hesitates on the threshold and asks, 'Am I disturbing you?'

My first assumption is that she works here, but even a superficial survey of her designer jacket, beautiful shoes and enviably expert blonde highlights tells me that she can't possibly be working here, and is very unlikely to be a fellow guest. At a loss, I stand and stare at her.

She eases gently into the room and comes out with the line that every ex-teacher dreads, 'You don't remember me, do you?'

Well, no, I don't. They change, our former students, they change out of all recognition, grow up, fill out, slim down, grow grown-up faces to replace the plump smoothness of their fledgling ones. We teachers are easy for them to recognise, already fixed in our adult selves in their memories, just a bit fatter or thinner, a lot greyer, a bit diminished.

'I don't,' I say. 'Sorry.'

'Well, I guess I've changed,' she says, and there is something about the quality of her voice that catches me. Can it possibly be?

'Irina?' I ask.

She laughs. 'Yes. Amazing, isn't it?'

I am not sure whether it is the coincidence of our meeting that she means or the transformation in her, but the transformation certainly amazes me. When I knew her fifteen years ago, she was chunky enough to be taken for a Russian shot-putter – big shoulders, muscly arms and a substantial bosom, which she emphasised by wearing padded gilets in startling colours. And then there was her hair. A victim of Soviet era dyes, I think, it had thinned to a fine, chemical orange fuzz, inadequate to balance the shoulders and the bosom. Now? Well, she must still have the infrastructure of the shoulders, but they are elegantly covered by her well-cut jacket, and must, I think, have lost some of their muscly padding. The bosom has certainly shrunk. And the hair! The hair is cut immaculately short, Jamie Lee Curtis-style, and highlighted and lowlighted in honey tones. Her skin, which I remember as pasty white, is glowing and gently tanned – the effect, I assume, of judicious exposure to Californian sun and plenty of moisturising.

I am speechless, more or less. 'Amazing,' I say, and we stand and look at one another, unsure how to proceed. Hugging is still a dubious business, and handshakes between women feel slightly ridiculous, so I just offer her a chair – the only chair in the room – and perch on the bed myself.

She looks round the room and I am immediately defensive; I don't want her to think that I can't afford better.

'Stourly isn't a place for luxury hotels,' I say.

She nods. 'This is very much like our rooms at the college,' she says. 'It reminds me of student days.'

Her student days are the subject that I very much don't

24

want to discuss, so I say briskly, 'Tell me what you've been doing since.'

She knows what I am doing, but concedes. 'I went back to Russia after... what happened, but I didn't settle. Being a doctor in Russia is no life. You worry about your NHS, but you have no idea. And it must be worse now that Putin is making his war.'

'So you went to the US?'

'Sure. On a student visa. I got the MSc that I didn't finish here at Marlbury.'

And along the way, I think, you finally learnt to use definite and indefinite articles – 'the MSc', 'a student visa'. You no longer think in Russian.

'Remind me what the MSc was on,' I say.

'Women's health. And then I was interested in nutrition and health for women, so I went on to a PhD in that field. My father died and I had some money.'

'And now you are giving papers at conferences.'

'Now I have a tenured post at Berkely,' she says. And she can't keep the triumph out of her voice.

'And you like California?' I ask.

She shrugs her elegant shoulders. 'What's not to like?' she says. And then she looks straight at me and says, 'Ceren is with me.'

Ceren? Turkish Ceren, Irina's fellow student whose traumatic experience led, in the end, to their whole group aborting their graduate studies and going home.

'With you here? Or in California?'

'Both, actually. She's a social scientist. She has an interest in cultural attitudes to GM foods.'

I am trying to formulate a neutral question but she forestalls me.

'We are together. She came to the US as soon as I had the money to pay for her studies.'

25

She is telling me something else too, I realise.

'Were you together when you were at Marlbury?'

'Of course. We hid it well because we knew Ekrem was spying on us all, but I believe he found out. What he did to her was supposed to be punishment, I think.'

I stare at her, and what I am thinking is that this woman is a killer and I let her get away with it, and I don't know whether what she has just told me makes that more defensible or less, and this is going to occupy my thoughts during a sleepless night, along with everything else.

'I didn't expect to talk about this, Irina,' I say. 'That was understood. In fact, it was understood that we wouldn't meet again.'

Irina doesn't react. Instead, she says, 'That police officer who was attacked, wasn't he the one who questioned us about Ekrem? *Scott*, I think I remember.'

I am not doing this.

'Well, I don't,' I say, and I get up from the bed. 'I've arranged to meet a friend actually, Irina, and I need to get ready. It has been lovely to see you and I expect we'll meet again.'

She can't do anything but get up too, and I take her arm and steer her to the door, desperate to be rid of her. 'Enjoy the rest of the conference,' I say, as I more or less push her out of the door. Then I lie down on the bed and shut my eyes.

She knows about David and me, I think. If the journalists were at my front door then they have my name, and in the absence of any information from the hospital or the police, won't they have padded out their stories with whatever they can find out about me? So for how long will I be safe here? How long before I am besieged here? How long before they throw me out?

There is a knock at the door. *Already?*

Freda comes cautiously into the room, and sees me on the bed.

'Has there been news?' she whispers.

I struggle up. 'No, no. No news – which they keep telling me is good news. I was just recovering from a visit from Irina Boklova.'

She sags with relief, and then becomes apologetic. 'She is a bit full on,' she says. 'I'm sorry I told her you were here. She sort of bounced it out of me.'

'I can imagine,' I say. 'They could probably have used her in the KGB. But it doesn't matter.'

She comes over, sits beside me on the bed and looks around.

'This is rather horrid, isn't it?' she says.

'I'm not here for a holiday,' I tell her. 'What's your room like over at the college?'

'Quite nice. But I'm sharing with Faith. We drew lots for the single room and Lisa got it.'

'I hadn't heard about Faith until I saw her in *Cymbeline* in the summer. Is she a new friend?'

'She's not in my year – she's the year above. I got to know her through doing props for *Cymbeline*.'

'She was a very good Imogen. Does she want to act?'

'I don't think so. She wants to do philosophy at uni. She's really clever. She got all A*s at GCSE. The school want her to try for Cambridge, but she's applying to Marlbury.'

'Living at home? That's not much fun.'

'She says it's the money.'

'More likely a boyfriend. Does she have one?'

'No-one serious.'

'Stepfather too mean to pay?'

'I don't think so. She seems to like him. And I thought he was quite nice until this afternoon.'

'What did he do? Did he upset you?'

This is what I am here for, isn't it – looking after Freda. And I am ready for it. I could just do with someone to shout at.

Freda laughs. 'He didn't do anything to me, but there was a terrific row, if you want to hear about it.'

Do I want to hear about it? Not much, to be honest, but Freda has brought me her story as a distraction, hasn't she? It would be churlish to turn it down.

'Tell me,' I say.

'Well, I didn't understand it all because it was about science, but I got the gist. It was your friend Dr Boklova who started it.'

'That figures,' I say.

And then she tells me the story – very well, actually: Irina's paper on GM foods and *nutritional advantage*, Hywel Jones challenging, a male/female stand-off, some nice verbal sketches of the elegant Indian, the neurotic American, a louche man called Kevin, who I have decided is a Mancunian, and the outraged post-doc dumped in the shit by Hywel Jones.

'Did he flounce out?' I ask.

'I don't think men do flounce, do they?'

'I think they flounce in their hearts.'

'Well, Dr Crawley stormed.'

'Good for him. What happened then?'

'They all had tea.'

'Of course they did!'

Freda looks at her phone. 'I have to get back,' she says. 'Set up for dinner.'

'Thank you for coming over. You distracted me for a good ten minutes. Do tell me if there is any follow-up.'

She kisses me and goes to the door.

'Oh, I forgot,' she says. 'Hywel Jones is also a groper.'

'Really?'

'Bottom stroking,' she says. 'Dr Boklova's friend. She threw a glass of water in his face.'

'Go, girl!' I say. And then a thought hits me. 'Was she dark – possibly foreign-looking?'

'Yes. Very pretty, actually.'

Ceren.

'Did Irina Boklova see what he did?'

'Yes. And she looked daggers.'

'Mm,' I say, and I feel a small chill of fear go down my back. 'Let's hope she hasn't brought any daggers with her,' I mutter as Freda closes the door behind her.

Chapter Seven

DNA

Sunday

Bloody Hell! Rula Bartosz woke and lifted her head from the pile of papers that had been standing in as a pillow. *Coffee,* she thought, and sat up and looked around, hoping none of the team had seen her. *'Can't let it get around that I'm not up to an all-nighter any more,'* she muttered, as she loosed her hair from its rubber band and tugged it back to refix it with ferocious tightness. Then she got up, stretched twice, and went to the coffee machine.

Coming back with a cup of dubious fluid, she reflected that there were no obvious natural ingredients in station coffee except the caffeine, and she supposed that was the point. She took a swig and grimaced. It was barely warm. They must be turning the machines off overnight now, and had only just turned them back on, she thought. *Efficiency savings.*

She sat back at her desk and picked up the sheaf of papers that she had been sleeping on – the forensics report that had come in two hours before. You had to hand it to Forensics, they could pull their plastic-gloved fingers out when they needed to. In fact, everyone had jumped to it as soon as the news about DSu Scott had got out. There had been no need to cancel weekend leave and call officers in – they were already volunteering in droves, and DCI Ireland was flying back from La Gomera to be SIO. A bit of her was disappointed, had hoped she might run it in his absence, but they weren't going to put a new DI in charge, were they? Not for the attempted murder of a senior officer. She thought, as she swallowed her revolting drink, that it wasn't just an attack on one of their own that had had people turning up for duty – people liked David Scott. He didn't go out of his way to win popularity as some did, but he gave people respect and he only lost his temper when they were genuinely crap. And he came down really hard on anyone disrespecting women officers – or women in general. Quite a lot of the women here fancied him; she had herself, until she realised that Gina was the only woman for him, however weird their relationship seemed to be. There was a story there, she felt sure. Why weren't they married, or at least living together? Was it what they both wanted – the distance – or was one of them just putting up with it?

She picked up another sheaf of papers – printouts from CCTV footage. You would think that outside HQ there would be good coverage, but it turned out not to be great. No camera covered the spot where the actual attack happened, but one had caught the probable attacker. Only two people seemed to have walked along there in the few minutes before the attack – a man and a young woman. The problem was that the angle of the camera meant that you could see the woman's face – girl's face more like – but not the man's. All that could be seen of him was the back of his head and neck – a white man wearing a beanie. But the fact that he was walking with a woman did support the story that the forensic evidence seemed to be telling.

Someone came into the room and she swung round, ready

to congratulate whoever it was that had arrived early for the team meeting, but it was DCI Ireland who was standing just inside the door.

'In early or staying late?' he asked.

'Tell me what day it is,' she said. And then she took in his spruce appearance. He didn't look like a man who had just got off a plane. 'When did you get in?' she asked.

'Five this morning. You get through pretty quick at that hour. Time for a wash and shave and a decent breakfast.'

He came over to her. 'Are you all right?' he asked.

She shrugged. 'Oh, you know...'

'Yep. What have we got?' He put out a hand for the CCTV printouts she was holding.

'I think this must be our perp. No-one else around at that hour, it seems.'

'So no witnesses. Forensics?'

'A bit. I think we've got his DNA, but no match on the system. But I've been thinking and I mapped out some lines to follow. But you may think different. I called a team meeting for eight, so here's the stuff, and over to you.'

She heard how grudging that sounded but she was too tired to play nice. She stood up, picked up the forensics report and dumped it in his hands.

He handed all the papers back to her. 'No you don't,' he said. 'What I want you to do, DI Bartosz, is lead the team meeting, and take us all through these while I get up to speed. Then I want you to go home and get some sleep.'

'I'm fine,' she said.

'You are not fine. You wanted to crack this before I got back. You have been here all night and there is a mark on your right cheek that was almost certainly made by a bulldog clip when you fell asleep at your desk.'

'That's clever,' she said. 'Have you ever thought of becoming a detective?'

He didn't smile. 'This is very personal to you, I know, and I'll give you as much responsibility as you can take, but you're no good without sleep. Tell us your thoughts, set us going on your lines of inquiry, and then go home.'

She could feel tears threatening and turned back to her desk. 'OK,' she said. 'Thanks.'

Nobody was late for the team meeting. Nobody rushed in at the last minute, clutching breakfast coffee. When Rula and Tom Ireland walked in, it was to an electric buzz of expectation and a restless need to be out and active. While Rula fixed blown-up CCTV images to a whiteboard, Tom Ireland spoke.

'First of all, thank you all for coming in. I know many of you have cancelled weekend plans, but I know too that you want to catch DSu Scott's attacker and this is where you want to be. DI Bartosz led you well yesterday, and she has some leads from forensics which came in overnight, so I am going to hand over to her. Any questions before I do that?'

'We'd all like to know just how long you were in La Gomera for, sir.'

The question came from the squad's self-appointed joker.

'Not counting time spent at the airport, three hours, DC Cotton. My wife is not happy. So, let's get this job done, and I might get back for a few days. DI Bartosz?'

He ushered Rula to take his place, and moved to the back of the room.

Rula looked out at the crowd of alert faces and felt a queasy moment of pride and panic.

'First of all,' she said, 'I have to tell you what you know already, that there are no easy answers. At that hour of a Saturday morning, very few people were about, and CCTV confirms that. And Forensics have picked up some DNA other than his own from David Scott's clothes, but there is no match on the system.'

She felt the room sag, and before energy started to drain away, she said, 'What is interesting, though, is that there were traces of the DNA of a third person – female – and microscopic specks of blood matching that DNA.' She turned towards the whiteboard behind her, and the CCTV images. 'These are the only images that the cameras picked up during the crucial minutes – apart from the images of David Scott himself, which I'll come to. As you see, the angle is bad for identifying the man, but the male and female DNA makes these two persons of interest at least.'

She looked out at the room and went on, 'Yesterday, we came up with four plausible scenarios for the attack, which were – what?'

'Random nutter,' a voice called.

'Yes, someone sleeping rough – psychotic episode. Plenty of homeless souls on the Embankment, but if these two on CCTV are who we're looking for, they don't look right. No baggage, too *couply*. And frankly, we don't want this to be the scenario because we won't find him. We had officers down on the Embankment yesterday morning, but what can they ask? *Seen anyone who looks a bit crazy recently? Know anyone who carries a knife?* They can go down again today but the dossers'll have moved on, out of the way of trouble. And Mark talked to the A&E staff at St Thomas's to see if they'd had anyone in with mental health issues who might be dangerous. They just rolled their eyes – like, *Everyone's pretty nuts these days, and that includes the staff.* But they did say that everyone who comes in gets searched, and there were no knives last night. So, other scenarios?'

'Targeting a police officer. Someone was waiting for the first officer to come in. Chose Saturday because it would be quiet.'

'Yes. And if he was the guy we have on camera, then he brought his girlfriend along either to admire or as cover – a couple hanging around doesn't arouse suspicion like a single man might.'

'But he could have been targeting DSu Scott specifically. If he'd been stalking him, he'd have known he always ran on a Saturday morning.'

The comment came from a bright, young, Asian woman, newly promoted to DS, who reminded Rula a bit of her younger self – alert, ambitious, impatient.

She said, 'And that would give us a narrower field, wouldn't it, Meera? I know you've been compiling a list of recent releases from custody – cases where DSu Scott led – emphasis on violent crimes. The problem is that now we've got the forensic report we know that the attacker hasn't ever been convicted. And they've looked at near matches, so it doesn't look as though he was taking revenge for a family member. But your work isn't wasted; we'll still look at those releases – especially where we think others were involved in the crime but we couldn't make a charge stick.'

She looked round the room. 'Any other scenarios?'

There was a silence, and then Tom Ireland said, 'I've only had a quick scan of the CCTV footage of DSu Scott's movements, but I would say there was an incident.'

'Because he changed his mind about crossing the road?' Rula asked.

'Exactly.'

She turned her attention back to the room to explain. 'The footage from the camera outside this building shows him running along the opposite pavement – where our suspect couple were walking – and then he starts to cross the road, about to come in, when he turns and starts to run back again. Then we lose him. But it looks as though something attracted his attention.'

'Maybe the guy just called out his name.' A suggestion from the back of the room.

'Maybe,' Rula said, 'though I'd have thought his copper's instincts would have made him wary of that. If he didn't know the guy.'

'What if it was the woman who called out?'

'Possible.' Rula took a breath. 'Something happened out there that stopped DSu Scott from coming straight into the building, and I think it will have taken more than just his name being called. Was something staged deliberately? What was it? And if this wasn't planned, the question is what that couple were doing there wandering along the Embankment at seven o'clock on a Saturday morning?'

'Going home from an all-night party?' DC Wayne Cotton called from the back.

'Possibly, but where would the party have been around here? You've got to be seriously rich and grown-up to live round here, don't you? None of us live nearby, do we?'

Meera Javid lifted a hand, like the good girl in class, and said, 'The house-to-house yielded nothing yesterday, did it? If this couple weren't local, should we be thinking about how they got here? We all know you can't park a car near here, but how about talking to staff at Victoria station – and Westminster underground? That early on a Saturday, there won't have been many people around, so they might remember.'

'A job for you, Meera. Yes.' Rula looked around the room. 'Any more ideas?'

The room was silent.

'OK,' she said briskly, feeling the energy begin to drain. 'Lines to pursue today: recent releases from custody, more local inquiries, interviews with transport staff, CCTV footage from the station cameras, more CCTV trawls – any cars being parked in a half-mile radius and any earlier sightings of our couple on their way. And –' she turned to Tom Ireland, 'what do you think about an appeal for the couple to come forward for elimination?'

He nodded. 'It's significant that they haven't already come forward as witnesses, but it'll confirm one way or the other.' He stood up. 'And now DI Bartosz is going home for some sleep, before she falls over.'

Rula said, 'Just one more thing. One of the paramedics who attended the scene says that DSu Scott said something before he lost consciousness. It was very faint, but she thought he said, "*Gotta hate*".'

An hour later, back home in Croydon, Rula climbed the two flights of stairs to her flat and felt her phone start to vibrate as she rummaged in her bag for her key. She fleetingly wondered whether, if there had been a development, she had the stamina to turn round and go back to the station. The call was not from the station. It did, though, demand almost as much stamina.

'Hello, Gina,' she said.

'Where the hell have you been? You were *unobtainable*.'

Rula closed her eyes and said, 'I was running a team meeting and then I was on the tube. Has something happened?'

'Nothing's happened. That's the point. I get nothing from the hospital, I get nothing from you.'

'But you will hear when there is anything to hear. We've heard nothing from the hospital, so we take that as good news.' She sounded as though she was talking to a fractious child, she knew.

'And what about you lot? What are you doing? Why were you on the tube? A senior police officer has been nearly killed right on your doorstep, more than twenty-four hours has passed and you've got nowhere. Why? Because it's the weekend and they're all mowing their lawns?'

Rula abandoned patience and decided that treating Gina like family was the only answer. 'Nobody's mowing their sodding lawn, Gina. We didn't have to cancel weekend leave – they all volunteered. The Met is getting a hammering from the media at the moment, and rightly – I'd be the last to say there aren't some subhuman bastards on the force – but we've got the good guys here – and some I wouldn't have guessed would give up their time.'

She thought of Wayne Cotton, who was never one to do more than he had to, and who, frankly, David thought was a waste of space.

'They are desperate to catch this guy, Gina,' she said. 'They have sat for hours and hours going bug-eyed watching CCTV footage. I've never known forensics get results back as quick as they have – people must have worked all night. And if it comes to that, the reason why I was on the tube was because I had been working for more than twenty-four hours non-stop and DCI Ireland sent me home for some sleep. And by the way, DCI Ireland has given up his annual leave and flew in early this morning. His holiday in La Gomera lasted for three hours. This is a bugger of a case – attack almost certainly by a stranger and no witnesses. Forensic evidence is limited because David is too sick for anyone to take forensic material from him. We can only use his clothes. No-one's going to give up and we will get the guy, but we're not doing magic here.'

There was silence at the other end, and she thought for a moment that Gina had hung up on her and her speech had been wasted.

Then Gina asked, 'They came in because they wanted to?'

'Of course they bloody did. Now listen, before I crash I'm going to call the hospital and tell them they have to talk to you. It may be that they have to give you a code or something so they know you're not a journalist or whatever, but I'll try to talk some sense into them – on condition that then you leave me to get on with my job. OK?'

A silence.

'OK,' she said.

Rula was about to ring off when a thought made her say, 'Just one thing, Gina.'

'What?'

'David was still just conscious when the ambulance picked him up, and he said something.'

'What?'

'The paramedic wasn't sure but he thought he said, "*Gotta hate*".'

'Just "*Gotta hate*"? As in, *Haven't you gotta hate it when someone kicks you in the head?*'

Rula thought she could hear the wobble of tears. 'He thinks he said *hate* twice. But it might mean nothing. He could have misheard,' she said.

'Do you know?' There was definitely not just tears but rage there now. 'Do you know, Rula? A while ago – on *Thought for the Day*, I think – I heard some pious optimist claim that love is stronger than hate in the world, and the evidence was that on 9/11, when people in the towers and on the planes phoned to leave their last message, they were all messages of love. Nobody used their last breath to tell someone they hated them. Only David. Only my so-called lover, Rula. What does that say?'

And then there was a violent clatter. From the sound of it, Gina hadn't simply rung off – she had flung her phone across the room.

Rula thought, '*Oh God. She was hoping he had left last words for her.*'

'*You've got him wrong, Gina,*' she muttered. '*He's a policeman. That was information. We just have to work out what it meant.*'

Chapter Eight

CATALYST

Sunday

Freda was not used to sharing a room; apart from a grisly couple of weeks at the beginning of COVID when she had shared a room with her brother because her step-grandparents were sleeping in her room, she had rarely done it. And Faith turned out not to be a restful roommate. She had woken Freda by tripping over something when she came back from the loo during the night, and now her laptop screen was glowing in the dark, spoiling the last ten minutes of dozing before Freda's phone alarm went off. She sat up.

'What are you doing?' she asked.

Faith continued to look intently at her screen. 'UCAS form,' she said.

'Do they have to be in already?'

'15th October is the deadline. And school wants them before that, by the end of this month.'

Something like panic hit Freda. This time next year, that would be her, making a decision that was going to affect the rest of her life, and at the moment she had no idea even of what subject she wanted to do, let alone where she wanted to go. But her panic was short-lived, swept away by the sound of running feet and the arrival of Lisa in a real state of panic. 'Faith,' she gasped, 'you've got to come!'

Faith looked up from her screen. 'I'm not on early duty,' she said. 'I did it yesterday.'

'No! No, it's your stepdad. You've got to come.'

'Why? What?' Faith was out of bed and putting shoes on.

'Just come!' Lisa said, and tugged her out of the room.

Freda stopped to put some shoes on and then ran after them.

Lisa led them down some stairs to the corridor below theirs – not one that Freda had been to before because it was Lisa's job to clean these rooms. Lisa stopped at a half-open door and pushed Faith inside.

'Look,' she said.

Faith went in, with Lisa close behind, and Freda held back, watching from the doorway. Her view of the bed was blocked by the other two, but she heard Lisa say, 'Can you feel a pulse? I couldn't feel a pulse.'

When Faith said nothing, Freda edged into the room.

'In the neck,' she said. 'That's supposed to be the best place.'

Faith stepped away from the bed. 'You do it then,' she said.

Then Freda could see Hywel Jones. He was very white and very still. Taking a deep breath, she approached the bed and felt inside his old-fashioned pyjama jacket, above his collarbone, for a pulse, as they had been shown in the first aid class she had done after GCSEs in the summer. His skin felt very cold and clammy, and she could see the sweat on his face. She couldn't find a pulse.

She stood back from the bed. 'We should tell someone,' she said.

The three girls looked at one another, and Freda thought fleetingly that they would remember this as a growing-up moment in their lives. There was no obvious grown-up to turn to. Alice, in the kitchen, was their boss, but she couldn't be expected to deal with this; there was a woman who worked for the college who had been around yesterday, but she didn't live there; and Hywel Jones was running the conference, and he was the one who seemed to be dead.

'I think we ring 999,' she said. And, feeling as though she was acting in a TV drama, she ran back to her room and picked up her phone.

It wasn't difficult, actually. The woman who answered did all the work. All Freda had to do was answer questions. She thought afterwards that it was surprising that the woman hadn't asked her how old she was, or why an adult hadn't called. Perhaps she had managed to sound grown-up.

Chapter Nine

PATHOGENS

Sunday

The wail of the emergency siren barges into my restless dreams and has me sitting up in panicky turmoil. It takes me a moment to identify the wail as an ambulance, and to work out where it is coming from. Then I go to the window and watch it parking in the forecourt of the college. My immediate thought is Freda. Logic should tell me that at the moment the college will be full of sedentary men in late middle age, far more likely to keel over as a result of a bit of overexcitement than a healthy sixteen-year-old, but I am beyond logic. A dark moon has risen, my luck has run out, there is nothing to stop the worst from happening.

With clumsy fingers, I text Freda, retaining enough sense not to sound panicky. *Ambulance?* I write, and leave it at that. Really, remarkably cool.

She texts back while I am watching from the window for her lifeless body to be brought out: *Something rather awful. Will tell you later. I am OK.* And I have to be content with that.

I resolved last night that I would not ring anyone until eight-thirty. It is Sunday morning. I will be reasonable. So,

I wash and dress and go downstairs to drink tea and eat two limp slices of toast with thin marmalade. Then I come back upstairs and phone Rula. When her phone tells me she is unavailable, I ring the hospital and feel that I am getting somewhere when I am told that I am being put through to the ICU. But there is no answer from the ICU; the phone rings and rings, taunting me with the possibility of contact. I call Rula again, but she is no more available than she was before. And so I sit there, alternating calls to the hospital and to Rula, until eventually she answers and gives me a bollocking. Which I deserve, because I made a stupid crack about the police all being at home mowing their lawns. But nobody tells me anything. Is it any wonder I am going nuts?

And now there's *hate* to deal with. I can't associate David with hate. I hate all sorts of things – places, people, attitudes, foods, clothes, weather – and I am vociferous about it, but I don't think I have ever heard David even use the word. I suppose he must hate paedophiles, and drug traffickers, and men who throw acid in women's faces, but I haven't heard him actually say so.

I sit at my window and look out across the road. It is quiet at the college. The ambulance has gone, and there is no sign of the drama that must be going on inside. In fact, there is drama everywhere. We are in dramatic times – not just war and floods and famine in the world, but here in the boring UK. This is 2022, the year of the three prime ministers, and a delusional woman has managed to get herself made prime minister, has killed off the Queen on their first meeting, and is now busy killing our economy. Panicky MPs are running round in circles looking for a responsible grown-up to take over and put it all right, and over-excited commentators are flooding the airways, claiming to decipher the Westminster runes. A lot of people, I realise, will be glued to televisions, radios, laptops and phones this morning, avid for news, but

I can't care. The world has shrunk to the inside of my head, and there is no room for anything else in there.

It is not long before I see Freda coming across the road, and I know I must rouse myself to a show of interest in whatever has happened at the college. When she comes in, I can't quite identify the look on her face, and then I think it is guilt. She is excited about what has happened and she feels bad about that. I recognise the feeling because I have had it myself.

'Dramas?' I ask.

'Awful,' she says, but before she embarks on her news, she asks about news of David.

'Zilch,' I say. 'I am just sitting here, waiting. Distract me.'

So, she tells me her story, and it is dramatic enough to hold my attention for a while. I let her talk before I ask any questions.

'Why did Lisa find him? What was she doing in his room?'

'She was on early duty. We're taking it in turns. Faith did it yesterday and I'm doing it tomorrow – if everyone's still here. We put out the breakfast buffet and get the urns going. Alice comes in a bit later to do the cooked food. We don't really do early morning tea, but he – Hywel – had asked Lisa to bring him a cup. Faith took him one yesterday. It was to do with his diabetes. He needed to wake up and do his insulin injection a while before breakfast.'

'Had he been dead for long? Did the paramedics say?'

'Not really. They did say there was nothing we could have done, though.'

'So, was it a heart attack?'

'I don't know. I don't think so. Faith told them about his diabetes, and they sort of nodded, as though that could be it. I didn't know – Faith explained – that too much insulin is as dangerous as too little.'

'But he was a scientist. He wouldn't be likely to get it wrong, would he?'

'No. Except – that row at the meeting yesterday, it was quite humiliating for him. It looked like he's lost the plot with his research. So I wondered if it upset him so that he wasn't concentrating...'

'Is that what Faith thinks?'

Freda shrugs. 'I don't know. The police are coming, apparently.'

'Really?'

'Professor Pratt has taken charge of things, and he says so. Standard practice with a sudden death, he says, but I'm not sure. He's called a halt to the conference, but no-one can leave until the police have been. They may want to question people, and we've got no idea how long that will take, so people are getting twitchy – particularly the ones with flights to catch.'

'When was the conference supposed to finish?'

'Tomorrow lunchtime.'

'But you girls need to be back at school, don't you?'

'Yes. Once the breakfast is out we're catching the train back. We won't be in time for assembly, but we'll be there for first lesson.'

I can see a car turning into the college courtyard. It is not a marked police car, but I am pretty sure that the man and woman who get out are police officers. Plain clothes, and I think I recognise one of them. This is more than routine.

'Look,' I say.

She comes over and looks out of the window.

'Police,' I say.

'Well, I'd better go back,' she says. 'I feel like an old hand at police interviews after last summer.'

'Don't try to be clever. That's what David would say. Why was it you who called the ambulance, anyway?'

'Somebody had to,' she says.

Chapter Ten

UNCERTAINTY PRINCIPLE

Sunday

'Why have they put a DI on this, if you don't mind me asking, boss?'

'I don't mind your asking, DC Matthews, but have you read our initial briefing?'

Ian Matthews concentrated on manoeuvring the car round a tight corner in a town not designed for cars, and then said, 'Chap in his sixties, diabetic, injected too much insulin, died in his sleep.'

DI Paula Powell looked up from her tablet and gave him an appraising look. She didn't know him well. He was graduate entry and a bit cocky with it, she thought.

'Two things,' she said. 'One, the observations of the paramedics and the initial pathologist's assessment both flagged up bruising near the injection site. Professor Jones had been a diabetic for quite a while – he was very unlikely to have bruised himself in the normal course of things. Two, it's an international conference going on at the college. World-renowned scientists. If we're going to interrogate them, they may feel a bit better about it if it's a senior police officer doing it. Plus – though the DSu may not be aware of this – I happen to have a degree in chemistry.'

'Really?' he shot her a look, as though reappraising her.

'A 2.1 from Marlbury University. What about you?'

'Psychology. Brighton.'

'Well, we're the dream team, aren't we?'

She went back to reading her briefing. 'He was found by three schoolgirls, working as domestic staff over the weekend. One of them is his seventeen-year-old stepdaughter, but another one phoned it in. She's – *oh my God!*'

'What?' he asked.

'Freda Gray,' she said. 'I know her – or know of her.'

'Has she got form then?'

'No, no. But she could be trouble. If it's the same Freda Gray, and it probably is. She lives around here. In Marlbury.'

'How do you know her?'

She took a breath. 'You've heard about DSu David Scott?'

'Of course.'

'Well, I know him quite well. I worked with him when I was DC. He's a brilliant officer and a lovely man.' She swallowed, fighting the wobble in her voice. 'But the point is, he's – in a relationship with Freda Gray's grandmother.'

He glanced at her. 'But he's not that old, is he?'

'Nor is she. Well, she's a bit older than him. She was his teacher when he was doing A levels. That's the source of the problem, I think.'

'What's the problem?'

'She fancies herself as an amateur detective and she thinks she has the right to muscle in on cases if she gets half a chance.'

'Well, she'll be in London now, won't she? If he's – you know…'

'Yes, she will. She lives in London anyway. But the

granddaughter is a chip off the old block. Thinks she's a crime-solver, too. Pretty full of herself.'

'How old, did you say?'

'Sixteen – and don't smirk like that, DC Matthews. You'll treat these girls with respect.'

He swung the car into the forecourt of the college. 'Yes, ma'am,' he said.

Paula looked around as she got out of the car. She realised that she had driven past the college often, but had never looked at it properly. If it wasn't genuinely old, then it did a good job of being fake old. It was a bit like an Oxford college, only more domestic, with the weathered brick building arranged around the grassed courtyard, and a stained glass window and impressive clock over an archway to further buildings beyond. A woman in a black jacket and trousers came through the archway. Paula saw her give a sharp look at their car, parked on the immaculate grass, and decide to say nothing. She advanced towards them, holding out her hand. 'I'm Anna Moulton,' she said. 'The college administrator.'

As Paula introduced herself and Ian Matthews, she considered the black outfit. Had she not been dressed when she got the news about Hywel Jones, or had she changed for the mood of the day? Had she expected to come in at all today, on a Sunday, with the conference in full swing? She could hardly have expected to have to deal with anything like this, but she was giving a determined impression of having things under control, only slightly marred by the fine sheen of sweat on her forehead.

'We have made a decision to cancel the rest of the conference,' she said. 'It was very much Professor Jones's project, so it felt only right. Of course, people are anxious to leave now, but I have explained that they need to wait until you have spoken with them.'

Paula and Ian Matthews followed her into the building.

'I have asked everyone to gather in the lecture hall,' she said, indicating a room to their left, from which came a steady rumble of voices. Paula glanced in. Chairs had evidently been moved from their rows and rearranged in groups around the large hall. The people sitting around looked like passengers at an airport, Paula thought, and some of them even had their luggage with them. The talk was fairly desultory and a lot of people were hidden behind newspapers. A few people were pacing, talking intensely on their phones. Others were texting or scrolling on phones. The atmosphere was edgy, and an explosion was likely if she didn't move fast with the interviews.

'How many people here for the conference?' she asked Anna Moulton.

'Sixty-one.'

'Then we'd better get started. Is there somewhere we can conduct interviews?'

'I thought the library – just at the end of the corridor.'

Paula turned to Ian Matthews. 'I'll start with the girls who found Professor Jones,' she said. 'Can you make a schedule for interviewing everyone else? I'm sure Ms Moulton can give you a list of delegates' names and where they're from. Start with the people with flights to catch.'

Anna Moulton ushered her into the library, commented that it was cold, fussed a bit with the radiators, and then left, taking Ian Matthews with her, and saying she would send the girls up from the kitchen.

'Would you like them to bring coffee?' she asked.

Paula accepted the offer. 'And I'll see them one at a time,' she said. 'Can you send the girl who found him? Lisa Baron?'

When Anna Moulton had closed the door behind her, Paula took a look round the library. In keeping with the style of the place, it was more like a gentleman's library in a country house than one designed for student use. There was a fake log fire in a fireplace with an elaborately carved surround, vases of dried flowers, and heavy, polished tables. She settled herself at one in the window alcove, which gave good light for watching faces. *Sixty-one people*, she thought. She couldn't do all the interviews, and she didn't think she could trust Ian Matthews to interview on his own. She got out her phone and called the station.

'Ideally, I want DS O'Malley,' she said. 'Or DS Saxon. Whoever is free first. And we need a WPC here too. I've got three traumatised teenage girls here, and no adult taking responsibility for them. Some of their parents will be here soon, I imagine, but we have a duty of care in the meantime.'

There was a knock at the door, and a girl came in, nervously balancing a tray of coffee things.

'Lisa?' Paula asked. 'Have a seat.'

The girl looked very young, her black skirt and white shirt looking more like school uniform than work clothes. She was pale and nervous, but Paula sensed a pulsing excitement as well in the alert brightness of her eyes. It was a reaction to tragedy that she was quite used to. Being a witness to a tragedy was shocking, but it was also dramatic – and it put you in the world of TV drama. Everyone now was familiar with the scenario – everyone thought they knew how this went.

She poured some coffee (a whole pot full – Anna Moulton knew this was going to be a long haul).

'Are you all right?' she asked.

The question took the girl by surprise. This was not the script she was expecting.

'Yes. Yes, thank you,' she said, and her pale face flushed pink.

'You've had a shock,' Paula said. 'Has anyone been looking after you?'

'Alice – she runs the kitchen – she made us all tea with sugar. I don't like tea, actually, but you know… It was much worse for Faith, though, so we've mainly been looking after her.'

'Would you like some of this coffee? You could fetch another cup.'

She shook her head. 'No, thank you. I'm all right.'

'Can you tell me exactly what happened this morning?'

'Yes.' The girl composed herself, and Paula thought she had probably composed her account in her head: a request from Hywel Jones the previous evening for an early morning cup of tea, the figure on the bed, apparently asleep, the failure to stir, even when she touched him, the panicky run upstairs to Faith's room.

Paula let her talk as she described the three girls running downstairs, and the urgent search for a pulse. 'Freda didn't come in at first, but when we couldn't find a pulse, she came in and tried – she's done first aid – and then she said she was going to ring for an ambulance.'

'You didn't think to find an adult to take charge?' Paula asked.

'We couldn't think who. Professor Jones had been in charge of the conference, and we get our orders from Alice, but she wasn't in yet – and anyway, we didn't think she would know what to do, really.'

'But Freda Gray did?'

'Yes. Well, she knows a bit. Her grandfather was killed – murdered, actually, last year – and Freda was there. I mean, this is different, I know, because Faith's dad wasn't murdered. It was his diabetes, wasn't it?'

'What makes you say that?'

She looked startled. 'Well, when Faith told them – the ambulance men – that he was diabetic, they looked at each other like – you know – that explained it.'

'I see.' Of course, the girls would have been talking about

it, and this was the view they would all have. 'Well, thank you, Lisa. I'd like to see Faith now. How is she?'

'She's OK. She's upset, of course, but we've been looking after her – me and Freda.'

'Ask her if she can come along for a quick word, will you?' Paula said, 'And tell her to bring a cup if she would like some of this very good coffee.' She watched as Lisa Baron sped out of the room.

Golden lads and girls, she thought. Where did that come from?

Faith Curtis must have been expecting to be summoned, because she appeared almost as soon as Lisa left. The first thing that struck Paula was that she looked more than a year older than Lisa Baron. The shock was evident in her face, but she was very much under control, composed and calm, and her voice, when she spoke, was surprisingly low and adult-sounding. Paula thought about the WPC she hoped would be arriving soon. She would need to be careful with this young woman and not patronise.

'Thank you for the offer of coffee,' Faith said, 'but I'm full of tea at the moment.'

'The solution to everything,' Paula said. 'I'm glad your friends have been looking after you, anyway. I'm very sorry for your loss.'

'Thank you.'

'Your mother is on her way here, I think.'

'Yes. I've spoken to her.'

'If you feel up to it, could you tell me what happened this morning? Lisa has given me her account but you may remember things she left out. Is that all right?'

'Yes.'

And she gave her account, which differed very little from Lisa Baron's until the end. 'I've been afraid of something like this happening,' she said. 'My mother and I both have.'

'You told the paramedics about his diabetes. Is that what you were worried about?'

'He had Alzheimer's. It was only diagnosed a couple of weeks ago, but he had been showing symptoms for a while – forgetfulness – and my mother and I were both worried that he would forget that he had already done an injection. There are safeguards you can use, but he was stubborn about it. He said muscle memory would see him through. He was in denial really.'

'What about your mother? How did she cope with it?'

'She's – was – very practical about it. Strategising about how to deal with it – how he could go on working – and looking up stuff online about how you can fight the dementia. And he was on some medication that was supposed to help. Neither of them was really acknowledging how bad it was. He hadn't told anyone at work, but they must have noticed things.'

Paula would have liked to ask more – about Hywel Jones's state of mind, about how he viewed the future – but these were questions more appropriate for Faith's mother when she arrived. But Faith had seen the body, so she asked, 'Did you notice any bruising on your stepfather, when you were trying to rouse him?'

'Bruising?'

'Yes. Anything at all?'

Faith shook her head. 'No. But we only felt for a pulse. He was – covered up.' Her voice wobbled slightly. *Not as composed as she wants to be,* Paula thought, and knew she wasn't justified in asking any more of this girl.

She said, 'Of course. The paramedics found an injection site on his arm, with some bruising near it. I wondered whether that was unusual.'

'It would have been until a few months ago. Long-term diabetics don't bruise themselves. But he has become clumsier, so...'

'Of course. Thank you for your help, Faith. That's all for now. I'm sure your mother will be here soon. Don't send Freda Gray in quite yet. Ask her to wait in the kitchen and I'll send for her.'

As soon as the door had closed, she called Ian Matthews. 'How's the schedule going?'

'Getting there, but I'm getting plenty of special pleading for an early interview – planes and trains, urgent medical appointments, children's concerts, sick dogs... you name it...'

'I'm sure you're coping,' she said briskly. 'Any news from the station?'

'Yes. DS O'Malley and a WPC are on their way.'

'Good. Send Bridget O'Malley in to me for a briefing as soon as they get here, and send the WPC down to the kitchen to offer TLC to the girls. And a heads-up: Hywel Jones had Alzheimer's. Early stage, very recently diagnosed. He hadn't told anyone at work, supposedly, but I wonder whether anyone had guessed. I'd like to talk to Professor Pratt right away, if you can locate him and send him along.'

Paula drank more coffee and ate a piece of shortbread, thoughtfully provided by Alice, she assumed. The Alzheimer's diagnosis made an accident more likely, but it meant that they had also to consider suicide. Everyone feared dementia, but for Hywel Jones his intellect had been his career. He might have been determined to fight the disease, as Faith had said, but he couldn't have expected much quarter from his colleagues if he was losing his grip at work. Could this conference have been his swan song? Was it possible that he had made a choice to kill himself here so that it wouldn't be his wife who found him?

With a peremptory knock, Peter Pratt came hurriedly into the room. He looked red-faced and slightly sweaty.

Not a coronary as well, Paula thought, and decided not to offer him coffee.

'Thank you for coming along, Professor Pratt,' she said, as soothingly as she could manage. 'I won't keep you long. I realise you must be busy. Do sit down.'

She waited for him to fuss with the position of his chair, and then went on.

'We are trying to get as clear a picture as we can of Professor Jones's physical and mental condition. We are waiting for autopsy results, but I wondered whether you, as a colleague, had noticed anything unusual, any sign that he was not well – aside from his diabetes, which we are aware of.'

Peter Pratt seemed to give an involuntary glance towards the door, as though he expected to find eavesdroppers. He cleared his throat.

'Hywel – Professor Jones – was always an excellent colleague,' he said, and Paula wondered if he was already planning his funeral eulogy, but then he went on, 'but we were all conscious recently that things were – not quite right with him.'

He stopped, almost as though he thought he had said enough, but Paula inclined her head encouragingly, and he went on, 'He was becoming rather forgetful – as we all can be under pressure, I know, but this was more. And his moods were uncertain. Hywel always had a bit of a temper – a fiery Welshman, you know – but it was getting more difficult to have a difference of opinion with him.'

'Did you raise these issues with him? It would have been difficult, I imagine.'

'Very difficult. But it got to the point last week when I felt I had to, as deputy head of department. The pressure of organising this conference was getting to him of course, but he was making things impossible for the staff who were trying to help – contradictory orders, mislaid files, and tantrums.

Really, I can only call them that – tantrums. So I asked our head of HR to join me and we sat down with him.'

'When was that?'

'Nearly two weeks ago.'

'How did it go?'

'Not well. He accused me of trying to get rid of him, of wanting his job. Some very unpleasant things were said.'

'And how were things left?'

'Hannah Johnson, the head of HR, calmed things down. I assured him of my support for this conference, and Hannah told me privately that she would press him to make a doctor's appointment. I don't know if he ever did that.'

Yes he did, and with the result that he feared, Paula thought.

'That's very helpful,' she said. 'I won't keep you any longer. For the moment.'

Peter Pratt stood up. 'I hope–' he said, and stopped and shook his head. 'Well, it's all very sad,' he mumbled, and bolted out of the room.

Chapter Eleven

BOILING POINT

Sunday

Meera Javid was exasperated. *Exasperated*, she told Rula Bartosz, not in her usual flat South London drawl, but with a pure, clipped precision that must, Rula thought, be an echo of her Indian mother's accent. It was probably a favourite word of her mother's, expressing her feelings about anything from untidy bedrooms to the poor quality of mangos at the market.

'I despair,' Meera told her, standing fuming in the doorway of her office. 'The best part of two hours spent going round those hell holes that are underground stations. Is it any wonder that I ride my motorbike to work? At least I get fresh air.'

And traffic fumes, Rula thought, but didn't say. She wanted to get Meera back on track, but Meera wasn't finished.

'I despair because they are all immigrants working down there, and they are such bad immigrants. They have no interest, they don't care. They didn't even know that a senior police officer was nearly murdered just nearby. They looked at me like it was nothing to do with them. With some of them it's a language problem, I think, but they're not trying.

They're the kind of immigrants who give immigrants a bad name.'

Rula knew that Meera wouldn't be offloading all this onto her if she hadn't known that Rula herself had an immigrant background. She sympathised, but this was no time for existential angst.

'So,' she said briskly, 'where to next?'

'I'm not giving up. Mainline stations may be better. I think all the stale air underground affects their brains.'

'Which stations?'

'I'll start with Victoria. I'll take the bike.' She zipped up her black leather jacket and left the room.

'Good luck,' Rula called, and turned to the forensic report on her desk. The hospital had allowed some swabs to be taken from David, but they had produced nothing very helpful, only the same DNA as they already had from his clothes. Just one thing was possibly helpful. There were traces of ink under his fingernails which had been identified as tattoo ink. It didn't get them far – London was awash with tattooed criminals – but it might make confirmatory evidence down the line. *A long way down the line,* she thought gloomily. They were nowhere yet.

She hadn't really been able to sleep. She had crashed out and woken, convinced that she had been asleep for hours, only to find that it had been two hours, so she had hauled herself back to work, to find DS Meera Javid at her door, complaining of her wasted morning.

The one thing she had achieved, from home, while eating a piece of toast, was some sort of rapprochement between the ICU at St Thomas's and Gina Gray, wherever she was hiding from the media. The report of David was still the same – *stable but critical* – but she now had a code word to give to Gina that should ensure that she could get that answer herself. She picked up her phone and rang.

'What?' Gina said.

'No real news, I'm afraid.'

'Following various lines of inquiry, blah, blah, blah.'

'That sort of thing. *Perspiration not inspiration*, you know.'

'Then why are you ringing?'

'I have a code for you.'

'What?'

'A password. You give it when you ring the hospital and you should be put through to someone who will talk to you.'

'I shall feel as though I'm in a le Carré novel.'

'I wouldn't know.'

'Really? Well, you're too young, I suppose.'

'Is that all right then? Take this down.'

'Wait a minute. A pen. OK. Fire.'

Having dictated the password and got Gina to read it back to her, Rula thought it might just be possible now to sign off as Gina's channel of information. Breezily, she said, 'So you can get what info there is first hand now. You won't need to call me, will you?'

'But you'll let me know if you get anywhere finding his attacker?'

'It's confidential information. Releasing it could damage the investigation. You'll know when we make an arrest.'

'Well sod you then!'

'Thank you so much for your help, Rula. Not at all, Gina, you're welcome,' Rula said.

'Sorry,' Gina said, sounding like a child who had been told to apologise.

'Where are you?' Rula asked. 'Are you avoiding the media?'

'Oh yes, no self-respecting journalist would want to be where I am.'

'Which is where? It might be useful for us to know.'

'I'm in Kent, staying at a very nasty pub. And now there's been a drama.'

'Really?' Rula was only half listening. In her sleep-deprived state, she was finding it difficult to keep focus. She really needed to get on.

'There seems to have been a murder. Well, an *unexplained death*, but a DI is here, and several other police officers, so I'm guessing suspected murder.'

'In the pub?' Rula felt her grip on reality slipping away.

'No, at a college across the road. A professor found dead in his bed.'

'How do you know?'

'My granddaughter is working over at the college – making beds.'

Granddaughter. Was there more than one? Rula remembered a granddaughter. Round about a year ago, David Scott had abandoned Rula in the course of an investigation – had left her in the middle of Leicester, whistled up a police helicopter and flown off to Scotland to rescue a granddaughter. *Freda,* she was called. If he hadn't arrested a murderer while he was up there, he would have lost his job.

'Would that be Freda?' she asked.

'You remember. Yes. She found the body.'

Rula closed her eyes. 'Why?' she asked.

'What do you mean?'

'Why is your teenage granddaughter making beds in a college? Why are you in the pub across the road? Why did she find a dead professor?' She could hear her voice running out of control and took a deep breath. 'Never mind. I don't need to know. Just tell me who's in charge of the case. I'm sure you know.'

'I've seen DI Paula Powell go in there. Do you know her?'

'I know of her. I've not met her. She worked on the case last year. You know, the—'

'She did, yes.'

Rula could hear David saying, *'Paula and Gina don't get*

on – a bit of history.' She didn't know whether to hope that this death would be distraction for Gina and make her own life easier, or to hope, in solidarity with a fellow DI, that Paula Powell could keep Gina out of it.

'Well, good luck, Paula,' she said.

Chapter Twelve

ACTUAL YIELD

Sunday

When Freda Gray arrived, she was carrying another tray, this one bearing a plate of sandwiches, a bottle of water with a glass, and more coffee.

'Alice says she knows it's early for lunch, but you might like to have these for when you want a break. The sandwiches are ham, but if you're a vegetarian she can make you some cheese and pickle.'

The sandwiches looked good – on granary bread with a herb garnish and posh crisps on the side – but the interview was going to happen first. Paula could not help suspecting that this was a ploy on Freda Gray's part, a bid to deflect her from questioning her as a key witness.

'Thank you,' she said repressively. 'Perhaps later. Put it down at the end there, will you, and take a seat.'

Freda sat, upright and neat in her white shirt and knee-length black skirt. She folded her hands in her lap, almost a parody of a model interviewee. Paula thought she might be taking the piss. She looked at the girl, scanning for similarities to her grandmother. Well, the last time she had seen Gina had been in the dark, in the pouring rain, outside a house where a murderer was burning evidence. She had not paid close attention to Gina's appearance. Anyway, it wasn't an actual, physical resemblance that was coming across; it was that irritating impression of knowing better, being smarter, running ahead of the game. Well, this was a sixteen-year-old, and Paula wasn't taking any shit from her.

'What are you doing working here?' she asked, and was satisfied to see the flash of surprise in the girl's eyes. She would have been primed by the others, would be expecting to give her account of finding the body, and would have her account nicely honed. *So we'll just shake things up*, Paula told herself.

'It's a weekend job,' Freda said. 'I'm old enough. I was sixteen last—'

'And how did you get the job?' Paula snapped.

'Faith Curtis asked me if I wanted to do it. She—'

'She's older than you, isn't she? How do you know her?'

'We worked on a play together in the summer. She was acting and I was working backstage.'

'Did you know her stepfather?'

'A bit. I'd met him a few times – just when he came to pick her up from somewhere. If we'd been —'

'What did you think of him?'

'He was nice. Friendly.'

'What did Faith think of him?'

'She liked… Why don't you ask her?'

'Because I'm asking you. Did she resent him?'

Freda raised her chin. 'No. Why would she?'

'Plenty of kids do resent stepparents.'

'I don't resent my stepfather.'

'Well, good for you. I'm asking you again, how did Faith feel about her stepfather?'

'She was fine with him; she was glad her mother had found someone after her father died. And he was very supportive.

He took an interest in her schoolwork. He got us this job.'

'OK.' Paula leant back in her chair. 'Why did you ring 999 this morning?'

'What?'

'Why did you ring 999?'

'I thought it was what you were supposed to do if...'

'If what?'

'If someone dies suddenly.'

'If you're only sixteen, you're supposed to let an adult deal with it.'

'There was no-one available.'

'There are sixty people at this conference – all of them adults.'

'Well, we couldn't just go randomly knocking on doors in the early morning. And the woman who answered my call didn't question my age.'

'How did you know he was dead?'

'I couldn't find a pulse.'

'And you're a medical expert, are you?'

'I've done a first aid course.'

'And did you meet any dead bodies?'

'No, of course not, but—'

'Most sixteen-year-olds would have rung their parents for advice, wouldn't they?'

Freda seemed to consider this. 'Maybe,' she said. 'I did think of ringing my grandmother, but she's got her own problems and I didn't want...'

And then Paula saw the tears come into her eyes, and felt a hot rush of shame. What did she think she was doing with this girl? She was just a witness – there was no possible reason to treat her as any sort of suspect – and she had her own troubles. David must be, if not a grandfather figure, then at least an uncle to her. Why was she being such a cow to her?

'I know about David Scott, of course,' she said, 'and I'm very sorry.'

Freda nodded silently and brushed the tears away with the heel of her hand, awkwardly, like a child.

'Would you like some water?' Paula asked. 'Or coffee?'

'I'm all right, thank you.' Freda sat up straighter and tugged her hair more tightly into its restraining rubber band. 'You can carry on interrogating,' she said.

'I think we're done,' Paula said, 'for the moment. Unless there's anything you want to tell me. Anything you noticed. Anything you think we should know.'

If Freda was surprised at the change of tone, she didn't show it.

'You mean when we found the – found Hywel?'

'Then, or at any other time. You're a bright young woman, you were around when the conference delegates were relaxing. Were you aware of tensions – personality clashes?'

Freda said, 'Actually, would you mind if I had some water? I'll bring you some more.'

Paula handed her the bottle and glass, and watched as Freda opened and poured. Her hands were shaking slightly, she noticed. Freda returned the bottle to the tray, took a swallow of water and sat with the glass held in her lap.

'There's an annoying guy who seems to like riling people. I don't know his surname. Everyone calls him Kevin.'

'In what way annoying?'

'A bit juvenile really. He seems to like being the centre of attention. And a bit gropey.'

'Gropey?' Paula asked.

'Free with his hands, you know. Although-' She stopped.

'Although?'

'Nothing.'

'Well, why don't you tell me, and I can decide if it's something.'

'I was going to say he wasn't the only one. There was something yesterday afternoon. Not many people saw it, but I was nearby. I was at the back of the lecture hall with the tea and coffee stuff, and glasses of water. One of the women was getting herself a glass of water before the talk, and Hywel came over and just reached out and stroked her bottom.'

'What did she do?'

'Threw her glass of water in his face!'

'Ha!' Paula couldn't repress a laugh. 'Who was she? Do you know her name?'

'I don't remember. I remember her badge said *University of California Berkely*. I guess women don't put up with harassment there. They bring law suits, don't they?'

'What did he – Hywel Jones – do?'

'I gave him a cloth and he mopped himself down and sort of tried to make a joke of it.'

'But you didn't see him being *gropey* with anyone else?'

'No.'

'Have you known him do anything like that before? With you, or any of Faith's other friends?'

'No. Never. I was really surprised.'

'And has anything else surprised you?' she asked.

'Well, I expect someone's told you about the row after the lecture?'

'Assume they haven't. Was this the same lecture?'

'Yes. It was about GM crops and nutrition and stuff. I didn't get a lot of the science, but Hywel was arguing against the lecture, and then he got challenged about his research results – something about some experiments he hadn't done.'

'Who challenged him?'

'Dr Varma. She's Indian, I think.'

'And it was actually a row?'

'Well, Hywel seemed to blame someone else for the experiments not being done, and the guy was furious and stormed out.'

'You don't know this guy's name, I suppose?'

'I don't remember. Something posh, I think.'

It would be interesting, Paula thought, to see whether anyone else volunteered an account of the row or the water-throwing.

'Well, thank you, Freda,' she said. 'I'll let you go now. Give my best wishes to your grandmother.'

She saw the girl hesitate, as though she might say something more, but she just nodded and slipped out of the room.

She was hardly out before Bridget O'Malley's face appeared at the door. She had obviously been waiting outside. Paula wondered how long she had been there and how much she had heard, shamed again by her earlier bullying. She was glad to see Bridget, anyway, who, despite her parody Irish name and matching pre-Raphaelite auburn curls, had a down-to-earth Midlands accent, and a manner to go with it.

'Yorright, boss?' she asked.

'Glad to see you, Bridget. Let's have a debrief. How are things out there?'

'Fine. DC Matthews is getting a hard time from the scientists. Everyone wants to be top of the list for interviews so they can scarper. He'd like us to talk to the Americans asap. He's finding them scary.'

'Poor little lad! How many Americans are there?'

'Five or six, I think. Two Californians and an older woman, who seems to have a group of minders, all clamouring that she is vulnerable and entitled to special treatment.'

'How vulnerable?'

'Health issues of some sort.'

'Well, we'd better see her first. I don't want anyone dying on my watch. I'm interested in the Californians, too. Did you get their names?'

'Yes.' Bridget O'Malley opened her notebook. 'A Dr Irina Boklova and Dr Ceren Alkan.'

'OK.' She pulled the tray of sandwiches towards her and offered it to Bridget. 'Help yourself. There are plenty.'

'What about DC Matthews? Should we keep some for him?'

'He'll get fed. Boys like that always do. I'm sure Alice won't let him starve. What's she like, by the way?'

'No nonsense. Not very touchy-feely, but she seems to have looked after the girls OK. WPC Lamb is there now, and she thinks they're all right. Lisa Baron's father is here, and wants to take her home. And Faith's mother has just arrived.'

'Aka Mrs Jones. Good.

'Actually, she's not Mrs Jones – she's Dr Curtis. She didn't change her name. But the point is, the girls are all right so we could send WPC Lamb back to the station.'

'No, we'll hold onto her. We've got sixty interviews to get through, and these aren't just witnesses, they're potential suspects. So we'll split them, and I'll have DC Matthews with me, and you can have WPC Lamb. I'll get Anna Moulton to find us another room. She's the college administrator.'

'I met her when I arrived.'

'Good. So we'll let the girls go home. No-one has come for Freda Gray?'

'Not as far as I know.'

And at that moment there was a quick tap at the door, and Freda Gray came in, carrying two glasses, another bottle of water and an extra coffee cup.

'Freda, you have a great future in catering,' Paula said.

Freda gave her a level look. 'I do hope not,' she said, 'but I have offered to stay and help Alice if Lisa and Faith are going home.'

'What about your parents? How do they feel about you staying?'

Freda flushed slightly. 'Actually, I haven't told them yet. There hasn't been time.'

She looked at their sceptical faces. 'My mum wasn't keen on me doing this job,' she said. 'I'll get a lot of *I told you so*.'

Bridget O'Malley laughed. 'She can't have predicted a death, surely?' she said.

'Well, no, but she's just a worrier. Anyway, I told my gran.'

'Gina?' Paula asked. 'But she's in London, I suppose.'

'Oh no,' Freda said as she went out of the door. 'She's just across the road.'

To Bridget O'Malley's obvious alarm, Paula leant over and beat her head gently on the table in front of her.

'Are you all right?' she asked.

Paula straightened up. 'No, I am not all right. Do you know who Freda's granny is? No? Then you haven't been paying attention. She is Gina Gray, and every journalist in the South East wants to find her because she is DSu David Scott's partner. She is presumably hiding out here, but she is someone you don't want anywhere near a police investigation. She is a smart-arse, a know-all and a busybody, and the last time I saw her she let her dog ruin my best coat.'

'I'd have thought she had enough to worry about just now.'

'Don't be too sure. If St Thomas's hospital and the Met have found ways of keeping her out of their hair, she will be looking for distraction.'

'You don't like her?'

'I find her extremely annoying. But to be absolutely honest, I find her annoying because she is quite often right. And at the moment I do feel sorry for her. The waiting for news must be hard.'

'But you'd like her to go back to London to wait.'

'I really would.'

She poured two cups of coffee and said, 'So this is the plan for this afternoon: I'll interview the Californians while you see to the other American – the fragile one – handle with care. Then you talk to her minions, and I'll take on anyone else who has an international flight to catch. After that, we'll look at DC Matthews's list and divvy people up. Having a surname starting in the second half of the alphabet, I always favour reverse alphabetical order. We're looking for anything they noticed, heard, wondered about – and anything that doesn't ring right in their stories, obviously. They're all going to say they were sound asleep, alone, in their own rooms, all night, but I'm interested in what happened during that day. Freda Gray told me a couple of things, and I'd like to know if anyone else mentions them. If you need to push, ask about the talk in the afternoon.'

Bridget O'Malley looked at her watch. 'Starting now?' she asked.

'Yes.' Paula was looking at a text which had just come in on her phone. 'Only, before I talk to anyone else, I'd better see Dr Ruth Curtis. I'll take a look in at the kitchen and collect her. I want to hear what she can tell me about her husband's state of mind.'

Bridget O'Malley gave her a sharp look. 'You're thinking suicide?'

'It's a possibility. That text was the results of the post-mortem blood tests on Hywel Jones. The insulin overdose was massive. Very difficult to see how it could have been accidental – even taking account of his dementia.'

'He had dementia?'

'Early stages of Alzheimer's. He hadn't told anyone at work. His stepdaughter told me just now.'

'So when you say you want to know if anyone noticed anything odd…?'

'Yes. Had anyone guessed? What sort of mental and emotional state was he in? We need a picture of him in those last hours.'

Chapter Thirteen

TRACE ELEMENT

Sunday

Rula Bartosz felt something almost maternal as she watched Meera Javid walk to the front of the meeting room. Meera had returned from her trip to Victoria mainline in a state of high excitement, but Rula had insisted that she report to DCI Ireland rather than spilling out her news on the spot. Now they were all gathered, and Tom Ireland had invited Meera to take the floor. She was loving her moment, Rula could see, as well as being terrified. The guys had just bloody well better not give her a hard time, she thought, or they would have Rula to deal with.

'You found a helpful witness, DS Javid,' DCI Ireland said. 'Tell us what you've got.'

Meera spoke up clearly and formally, and Rula heard the eager schoolgirl in her again.

'I had no success at the underground stations,' she said, 'but at Victoria mainline station I encountered a very promising witness. It was not easy because if station staff work Saturdays, they don't work Sundays, but the witness in question was working extra shifts because he is saving up for his daughter's wedding.'

Come on, Meera, stick to the point, Rula thought, and found that she was making a discreet *get on with it* wheeling motion with her hand.

Meera had caught the gesture. 'I tell you this,' she said, 'because I want you to understand the kind of man he is – a family man with daughters, a man who worries about the vulnerability of young women and girls. He is Mr Mark Small, and—'

'Isn't he one of the Mister Men?' called out a voice from the back. It was Wayne Cotton, of course. Rula looked at him, lounging at the back with his admiring sidekicks. There was something piggy about him, she thought: he wasn't fat yet, but he had the beginnings of a beer belly, and he had a piggy face, with sharp little eyes, chubby cheeks and a squashed, piggy nose. He swaggered around, looking at the women officers as if he could have any one he chose, only they weren't good enough for him.

Meera was unfazed. 'I expect he's heard all the funny jokes already, don't you?' she said, coolly. 'The point is, he is alert to the possibility of people trafficking. He has been on a course.'

Rula tensed, waiting for the jeers and whistles that *been on a course* usually produced from the back row cynics, but they were silent. They knew that Meera had something to tell them.

'He recognised the girl who was caught on CCTV,' she said. 'She and a man came off the first train from Dover yesterday morning. There were not many people coming through at that hour on a Saturday, so he had time to notice, and they worried him.'

'Specifics?' DCI Ireland asked.

'Body language. He had hold of her hand, but not like boy and girlfriend – he had her arm bent upwards.' She demonstrated with a clenched hand held close to her body.

'And he was white and she wasn't. We could see that from the CCTV – she's Asian or Middle Eastern. Actually, Mark Small said she was my colour. He spoke to her. He was on duty by the exit – where you put your ticket in – and he spoke to her as the guy was getting their tickets out – he commented that they were making an early start and it was still quite chilly. She had a thick, padded jacket on, and he said that must be cosy – but she didn't respond. He thought she couldn't understand him. He tried the trafficking sign. You know.' She demonstrated the sign: palm up, thumb tucked in, fingers clamped down. 'But no response, and the guy shoved their tickets into the machine and pushed her through.'

'What was the man wearing?' Rula asked.

'That was something Mark Small noticed. They were wearing very different clothes. You know how couples often wear the same sort of style, well these two didn't. She was in old-looking jeans and scruffy trainers, and the thick jacket that looked too big for her, and he was all in black – black jeans and T-shirt, and no jacket.'

'Maybe he'd lent her his jacket.'

'Mark Small didn't think so. He said it looked quite stained – not smart enough for the guy.'

'What about his face? Would your witness be able to help with a photofit?'

'He thinks so. Thirtyish, white, designer stubble. Wearing a beanie, though, so he didn't see his hair. And dark glasses, which he thought was odd on the underground.'

Meera looked round at Tom Ireland.

She wants a gold star, Rula thought, as Tom Ireland took her place at the front, dismissing her with a brief, 'Thank you, DS Javid.'

He looked round the room. 'Any thoughts?' he asked.

The room was quiet, and Rula guessed that, like her, they were all looking for the solid nugget of fact. She spoke.

'So the scenario that's being suggested here is that the girl, who is possibly foreign, is being coerced. That the train started in Dover raises the possibility of trafficking – that the man is involved in the boat crossings, or has a deal going with the boat owners and picks up girls and brings them to London. But they could have got on the train anywhere between Dover and London, couldn't they?'

'The stains on her coat might have been seawater,' a voice called.

'They might and they might not,' Rula said. 'Well, if we go with that scenario for the moment, then where was he taking her when they were caught on CCTV?'

Her question seemed to release them, and suggestions and objections started flying.

'To a nail bar, and on to a knocking shop.'

'A bit upmarket round here for that.'

'There are knocking shops everywhere.'

'Or a club.'

'Plenty of big houses where they want cheap domestics.'

'But why take her right past here? Wouldn't he avoid any police station, let alone Met HQ?'

'Showing off? Letting her know she can't expect help from the law.'

Tom Ireland cut in. 'Let's follow that trail. He picks her up in Dover, and he's got somewhere round here to take her. It makes him feel like a big man to walk her past here. How does he encounter DSu Scott? We have the idea that he called out to David Scott as he was crossing to come into the building. Why would he do that? That's taking bravado too far, isn't it?'

'Unless the girl called out,' Rula said. 'She may not have understood much English, but *Police* is pretty generally known, and she would probably know how to shout *Help*.'

Tom Ireland stepped in. 'There's a lot of conjecture here,

but we definitely need to track this couple down. Why haven't we found them on CCTV between Victoria and here?'

A DC spoke up. 'We have her in a couple of places, but he is always turned away. We can't get his face. Almost like he knows where the cameras are.'

'Which sounds like a pro,' Tom Ireland said. 'But we haven't got his DNA, so he's a good one. Let's try to find out where the girl has got to. They were on foot, so let's assume they weren't going far. Try everywhere that the girl could have been put to work. Take the CCTV images with you. And knock on the doors of millionaires' mansions again, and ask about domestic staff. Advise co-operation. Tell them if they don't hand the girl over now and we find her later, they'll be facing a prison sentence. Aiding and abetting attempted murder. Put the fear of God into them.'

He looked round the room. 'Any questions? No? That's it then. Good work, DS Javid.'

And Meera Javid bowed her head to hide a wide, wide smile.

Chapter Fourteen

COHESION

Sunday

I have used the password! I felt completely ridiculous when I rang the main switchboard and said I had been given a password. I felt as though I should be calling from a red phone box, and at the same time I fully expected the receptionist to ask me who had been pulling my leg. Instead, she simply said, 'Thank you. Putting you through,' and the next moment a brisk voice said, 'ICU.' I was so flustered that I stammered and babbled, but I got an answer: *David* (why do I mind this familiar bandying of his name so much?) was still critical, but he was stable and had passed a comfortable night.

At this point I regained my wits.

'But he is still in a coma?' I asked.

'Oh, yes.'

'So how can you possibly know whether his night was comfortable.'

'We monitor very closely,' she told me. 'We are aware.'

'Because he's wired up to machines?'

'Yes.'

'I want to see him,' I said, before I knew I was going to say it.

'We don't advise it at this stage. It will only distress you. But we can let you know of any change. Do we have your details?'

'Probably not. I don't suppose the harpy on triage duty passed them on.'

With obvious forbearance she took my name and mobile number, and I was left with no more knowledge and no-one to shout at.

So, I am back at my window, watching for comings and goings across the road. I have seen a woman with a professional look about her park a small car and walk into the college – possibly connected with the police, I suppose – and then, when am thinking that I can't just sit here, and it is getting on for two o'clock, and I probably ought to eat something, I see Freda come out and run across the road.

'Is there any news?' she asks, as soon as she is through the door.

'I was able to talk to an actual nurse. I have a secret password.'

She giggles, because although disaster is all around, you have to laugh, don't you?

'What did the nurse say?' she asks.

'The same. He's still in a coma. *Stable but critical.* And he had a comfortable night.'

'How can they tell?'

'That's what I asked.'

'What did she say?'

'Their machines tell them.'

She considers this for a moment. 'I don't think I believe that,' she says.

'Neither do I.'

She perches on the bed next to me, and says, 'Could you cope with a distraction, do you think?'

'What sort?' I ask, immediately resistant.

'Faith's mum is here, and she's seen DI Powell, and she's really unhappy about the line the police are taking.'

'And you think I can influence Paula Powell! I'm the last person. She really doesn't like me.'

'She sent her best wishes.'

'So she's made the connection between us, has she? I suppose she was bound to. Well, that's kind of her, but she still doesn't like me.'

'Why not?'

'I think it's because she's always fancied David, but it may just be that she finds me annoying. Some people do.'

Freda gives me a huge grin. 'I know,' she says, 'but you are very lovable really.'

'That's what people say about their dog when it has just nipped your ankle.'

We are silent for a moment, and then I ask, because I can't resist, 'So what line is Paula Powell taking?'

'Suicide. A deliberate insulin overdose.'

'Why?'

'He had Alzheimer's – he had just been diagnosed – and then – the thing is, I feel it's my fault.'

'His suicide? How —'

'No. That the police think it was suicide. I told DI Powell about the bottom-stroking thing yesterday, and about the row over Dr Boklova's paper.'

'I'm sure other people must have told her too. They were all there. And you don't kill yourself because someone throws a glass of water in your face.'

'No, not if there's nothing else, but I suppose if you put it all together…'

I am assailed by the lurking dread that I have been suppressing ever since I saw the police car draw up this morning.

'Freda,' I say, 'did Dr Boklova see the water-throwing?'

'Yes. She was up on her podium getting her stuff ready for her talk, so she was facing our way.'

'And did she react?'

'Yes. For a moment she looked really furious. I think it was like a feminist thing – with them coming from California.'

I could tell Freda that they are lovers, but I don't. Instead, I say, 'So she's quite likely to have told DI Powell about the incident, isn't she? You just did what you were supposed to do and gave the police information. What they do with it is not your problem.'

'But it is,' she protests. 'Because now they're fixed on suicide, and Faith's mum is so upset. She says he would never have killed himself – it was against his principles.' She looks at me. 'So I said you might be able to help. I thought, as you know DI Powell, you might be able to talk to her.'

'Honestly not,' I say. 'I'd only make things worse by interfering.'

Freda looks stricken. 'The thing is,' she says, 'I told Faith's mum that I was sure you could help.'

'Well, you shouldn't have done,' I say, more sharply than I mean to, and then I relent, because Freda has had a horrible morning and deserves some credit for worrying about someone else.

'Would it help if I had a talk with Faith's mum?' I ask. 'It would at least give her a chance to offload.'

'Would you?'

'I need to eat some lunch and I can't bear to eat here. I could take her to the café down the road. She probably doesn't feel like eating, but she might like a cup of tea.'

Freda jumps up. 'I'll go and get her,' she says. 'You'll like her. She's a lecturer at Marlbury Uni.'

'What's her name?'

'Ruth. Dr Ruth Curtis. She didn't change her name when she married Hywel Jones.'

She rushes off and I get up and make moves to smarten myself out of my morning stupor. I remember Ruth Curtis from my days at Marlbury, and she was a nice woman. I gave English tuition to a Columbian PhD student of hers who was struggling with writing his thesis. I learnt more about the travails of the Columbian coffee industry than I have ever wanted to know. But if food production is in her area of expertise, then I wonder why she hasn't been at this conference, and how much she was aware of her husband's problems in keeping a grip on his research.

I have just given up on getting my hair to do anything orderly when Freda arrives with my lunch date. Ruth Curtis is wearing grey trousers and a navy blazer. I am always interested in what we choose to put on in moments of crisis. She is wearing work clothes. Calm efficiency is what she is aiming for, and pretty much succeeding, though the ravages of tears are hard to disguise except in the very young.

We shake hands, acknowledge that we know one another of old, and exchange condolences. I am having to accommodate to the idea that not only does the world know about the attack on David, but it also knows about me. *Get used to it,* I tell myself.

I lead us downstairs and past the malodorous dining room, and head down the road to my café. Ruth looks reassured by the cosy warmth of the place, and I am delighted to find that our waitress today is French. It is rare enough to find Europeans serving you these days, since the great Brexit exodus, but a French waitress is positively exotic. She has that slightly detached French manner, as though floating above a milieu that is not quite good enough for her, but when Ruth says she doesn't think she can face eating anything, and is already awash with tea, she looks at her gravely and suggests a *café au lait* and a small slice of cake. 'Cake is very comfortable,' she says. I wonder if she means *comforting*, but *confortable* in French is pretty much congruent with *comfortable* in English, so I think she knows what she means.

I want to give Ruth time to open our conversation in her own way, so I amuse myself with thinking about the place of cake in times of crisis. I have a friend who likes always to have some fruit cake in a tin *in case of emergencies*. She just means unexpected visitors, but I think about Alessandro yesterday, and the healing properties of almond cake. There is a PhD topic to be had here, I feel. The French may have Proust's everlasting madeleine, but *The Role of Cake in the English Novel* looks promising to me.

Our food and drink arrive promptly. Although I am quite hungry, I have decided, since it is now two-thirty, that lunch has escaped me, and I have ordered cake too. Lemon and poppy seed, to be precise, as recommended by our waitress. It is moist and delicious, and our coffee is smooth and fortifying. I am pleased to see Ruth cut her cake into squares and then start to eat them, almost without noticing she is doing it, as she begins to talk.

'Freda tells me that you know Detective Inspector Powell,' she says. She has a soft voice, her accent anglicised American.

'Only slightly,' I say. 'I found a body on the beach some years ago, when I was living on the coast. She was in charge of the investigation.'

I don't mention the other cases – one of my students murdered in the university library, a pupil of Ellie's pushed down stairs, my Iranian students witnesses in a gangland killing. I don't want her to think I am weird, after all.

'What do you think of her?' she asks.

I hesitate. 'Well, she doesn't like me,' I say, 'so I'm not impartial, but I think she is pretty able, if a bit unimaginative.'

'Do you mind if I ask why she doesn't like you?'

'She thinks I'm a busybody. And I am.'

'I think that's what I need,' she says. 'She's wrong about my husband's death and I need someone to tell her so. She won't listen to me.'

'I'm afraid she won't listen to me either. She's not much of a listener.'

'How much has Freda told you about my husband?' she asks.

I feel embarrassed to admit that Freda has been giving me information, but I can't help without it, so I say, 'I know he died in his sleep, apparently of an insulin overdose.'

'That's the thing!' she exclaims, raising her voice for the first time. 'As soon as anyone hears *overdose*, they think *suicide*, but Hywel would never have killed himself. We talked about it. He was brought up as a strict Welsh Baptist, and he believed that suicide was a sin. He had a diagnosis of Alzheimer's last week, yes, but his reaction was that this was God's will, but that God would expect him to do everything possible to live well with the disease. He was already on medication to slow down the progress of the disease at this early stage, and he was researching new treatments. We were thinking about going to the States, where there are a number of trials going on. I have family there, and they would put us up. He was very positive. Killing himself was the last thing he was thinking of.'

'So you think it was an accident?' I say.

She frowns. 'The trouble is, I don't really believe that either. And stupidly I told Inspector Powell that, which sent her galloping off on the trail of suicide.'

'The dementia?' I say. 'Couldn't that have made him confused, so he injected too much insulin?'

She picks up her coffee cup and sits holding it, as if for comfort on a cold day. 'He wasn't at that stage of dementia – and he had been diabetic for a long time. He used to say injecting was muscle memory.'

'All the same...'

'How much do you know about diabetes?' she asks.

'I know there are two types – one and two – and that type one diabetics have to take insulin.'

'Do you know what the insulin does?'

'Not really.'

'Inspector Powell has a degree in chemistry, I discovered. So she's on it.'

For a moment, I am furious. It's as though Paula has cheated, suddenly pulling a chemistry degree out of her sleeve.

'Well, my degree was in English,' I say rather sharply, 'so I understand hard words, but you'll need to explain the science.'

She puts her cup down. 'It's not complicated,' she says. 'Diabetics need to take insulin because the pancreas isn't producing it naturally. And insulin is needed to turn glucose into energy. When we eat carbohydrates, the body breaks them down into glucose, which goes into the bloodstream. If there is no insulin, then glucose levels just get higher and higher, because it's not being converted into energy and used or stored. Untreated, that will kill you.'

'So, if you inject too much insulin?' I ask.

'Then your blood sugar level will go too low, and that's dangerous too. No glucose going to your brain, and you will die.'

'Wouldn't it be quite easy to inject too much?'

'No.'

I can see that she is in full teaching mode now. I am expecting diagrams.

'Why?' I ask, the keen student.

'He has two types of insulin and two syringes – they're called pens actually. They don't have the long needles like you have for other injections – they have little, short needles and you press a button to release the insulin. During the day, diabetics inject before meals, using short action insulin. There is a dial on the pen which controls how much they inject, and Hywel would sometimes adjust that, according to how much carbohydrate he was expecting to eat. So, in a restaurant, he might take an extra unit if he was planning to have pudding, for example.'

'Right. So he could have made a mistake in the adjusting and—'

'No! Wait!'

She almost shouts. I am a disappointing student.

'Hywel's overdose was of his night-time insulin. That is a slow-action insulin that stops the blood sugar level from going up too much overnight. That has a dial on it too, but Hywel never altered that. He'd settled on the amount that suited him, and did the same amount every time.'

'Couldn't he have forgotten he'd done it and then done it again? Is there any way of checking if you've done it? It must be difficult to remember something you do automatically every day. Like remembering if you have locked the car.'

'There isn't any way of checking – though I think there ought to be. Diabetics develop routines as a fail-safe. So, for example, when Hywel injected before a meal, he left the pen out on the table, so he knew he'd done it. He couldn't do that in restaurants, really, and sometimes he would ask me if he'd done it or not. Even before the dementia. As you say, it's so automatic you can forget.'

'So,' I say, 'couldn't he have woken in the night and thought he hadn't done the night-time injection, and done it again?'

'No. Because that's not what happened. The police found that night-time pen beside his bed. The dial on it had been moved right up to the highest level – far higher than his usual dose.'

'And you don't think he could have moved it?'

'His dementia was only just starting – he was forgetting names and appointments and where he had left things – but he was still coping with routines. He brought me my breakfast in bed every morning, because he was an early riser, and there was never anything wrong with it.'

I have one last go. 'He was staying in a strange place,' I say, 'and you weren't with him. Mightn't that have affected his behaviour?'

For answer, she sighs and sits back in her chair. 'It might. And I have to think that's what happened because the alternative is worse.'

'Meaning suicide?' I ask.

'No. I know it wasn't that, and there is only one other alternative, isn't there?'

We look at each other. Neither of us is going to say *murder*.

Eventually, I say, 'Someone else did it?'

She nods. 'And who could possibly want to do that?' she says. 'Hywel could be annoying – a bit pedantic – but not so anyone would want to kill him.'

But he was a groper, I think. *Perhaps worse. Did you know that?*

At this point our waitress comes over and offers us more coffee. We decline, and I ask for the bill. She looks at Ruth's empty plate and says, 'You hate it.'

Ruth looks startled and starts to say, 'No, I—'

I understand what is going on, though, and cut in quickly. 'Yes, we both ate the cake. It was delicious. A good recommendation.'

Satisfied, the waitress goes off to get our bill, and Ruth whispers, 'I thought she said, *hate it.*'

'She did. Hypercorrection. In French you don't aspirate initial 'h', so when French speakers are speaking English they have to remember to do it – *hospital,* not *'ospital,* and so on.

86

But then there is a danger of overcorrecting, so they put '*h*' before a vowel when there isn't one. Peter Ustinov does it beautifully when he is being Poirot. "*I keep my heyes hopen*" he says in *Death on the Nile*. Perfect.'

Ruth is looking at me with polite incomprehension. 'It's not a film I've seen,' she says. 'I'm not keen on whodunnits.'

And possibly not on linguistics either, I think.

We are quiet on the way back to the college, where I leave her, saying I will see what I can do about talking to Paula Powell, but promising nothing. I don't say again that Paula doesn't like me, because it feels childish somehow, but I burble about the police having their own way of doing things, and leave it at that.

I leave Ruth at the college gates, but can't face returning to my nasty little cell, so I go for a walk round the streets of Stourly, chewing over my dilemma and muttering to myself as I dissect my conflicting imperatives in a sort of Socratic dialogue with myself.

Q You know that Irina Boklova killed a man in the past, in Ceren's defence – and Ceren was complicit in the killings. How can you justify not giving that information to the police?

A Paula won't believe me. Another man was convicted of that murder. He was a professional criminal and had committed at least one other murder, so it didn't seem to matter.

Q Is that your real reason – that Paula won't believe you?

A Of course not. Look, either she doesn't believe me or she does, and then she'll have to reopen the case, and I'll be charged with all the things they charge you with if you haven't been helpful. Paula would probably throw in conspiracy to murder as well, if she thought she could make it stick.

Q So there's a moral dilemma?

A Of course there's a bloody moral dilemma.

Q Do you believe that murderers should be punished?

A Of course I do.

Q So why didn't you tell the police what you knew about the murder of Ekrem Yilmaz fifteen years ago?

A You know why.

Q Spell it out for me.

A He'd raped Ceren and he was threatening to come back for more. He had her in his power. She couldn't tell anyone because he was a Turkish government agent and would be protected, and he would make sure that all the blame and the shame would be on her.

Q And you think that's justification for murder?

A They didn't plan to murder him. They wanted to threaten – to scare him off – and they panicked, and it got out of hand.

Q You believe that?

A I did at the time.

Q And now?

A At the time I didn't know that Irina and Ceren were lovers. There were five women involved. Irina was the leader, but I didn't know how personal it was for her. I thought of it as an act of sisterhood.

Q High-minded?

A If you like.

Q And now?

A I'm not sure. I don't think love can be a moral imperative.

Q Interesting word, imperative. What do you know about Emmanuel Kant?

A Now you're going to hit me with the categorical imperative, aren't you?

Q I think it's time. Just spell it out for me.

A It's an unconditional moral obligation that holds for all people at all times.

Q Very good. And not helping someone to get away with murder is one of those?

A I suppose so?

Q That won't do.

A All right. Yes.

Q So what are you going to do?

A Oh, sod off, Emmanuel, you sanctimonious prig.

I have been muttering furiously to myself, but I must say this more loudly than I intended to because a woman walking towards me looks alarmed and crosses over the road. I continue my walk and end up at the college gates.

Chapter Fifteen

ACTION POTENTIAL

Sunday

Paula Powell ushered Dr Ceren Alkan out of the library and was surprised to find Dr Boklova, whom she had interviewed earlier, hovering outside the door, waiting for her colleague. And not just waiting but ready with a protective arm, a whispered *'Are you OK?'*, and a baleful look at Paula – for all the world, Paula thought, as though she had been applying thumbscrews to the woman, rather than taking her through a gentle rerun of the previous afternoon's seminar and its preliminary water-throwing. She watched them walk away from her down the corridor and was about to go back into the library when someone came rushing past them, heading in her direction. It was a woman, and Paula recognised – with no surprise at all, really – the figure of Gina Gray. She was less dishevelled and rather better dressed than the last time she had seen her, but there was no mistaking her, or the air of busy importance that she carried with her.

'Paula!' she called as she bore down on her.

'Who let you in?' Paula demanded, as she tried ineffectually to block the doorway.

'Came in through the kitchens. My granddaughter's working here – but you must know that.'

Somehow she was past Paula and in the library, looking around appreciatively. 'Nice place,' she said. 'They do themselves well here, don't they? Oh, hello.'

She had noticed Ian Matthews, sitting at the table, writing up notes on the interview with Ceren Alkan.

'DS Matthews, Mrs Gina Gray,' Paula said tersely. 'So you know this place, do you?'

'Used to teach here a bit in my Marlbury Uni days – which is what I need to talk to you about.'

'About teaching here?'

'About my Marlbury days and those two I just passed in the corridor.'

'Dr Boklova and Dr Alkan?'

' You know who they are, don't you? You must remember them.'

And there it was. That was why she couldn't stand the woman. She made her feel stupid and she did it deliberately. Well, sod that. She wasn't going to look stupid in front of Ian Matthews, who had, she was sure, been enjoying their exchange.

She went back to her place at the table and indicated the chair facing her. 'I'm very busy,' she said, 'so if you have information that you think is relevant to this case, I'd be glad if you would keep it brief and factual. Sit down, please.'

And she watched as Gina seated herself in the chair with exactly the same mocking compliance as she had received from Freda earlier. *A chip off a very old block*, she thought, spitefully.

She rearranged some papers on the table in front of her, giving herself thinking time, and said, 'We know, of course, that Irina Boklova and Ceren Alkan both studied at Marlbury University for a short while, but—'

'But both left early, without completing their course,' Gina interrupted. She leant forward and said, as though encouraging a backward child, 'And why was that?'

'I don't know,' Paula said, 'but I assume that you think it was connected with the death of Mr Yilmaz.'

The name had come to her just in time. She couldn't dredge up his first name but the surname had stuck because the victim and the killer had the same one – were cousins, in fact. She looked at Gina. Was that a flicker of disappointment that she had remembered the name?

'Ekrem Yilmaz,' Gina said. 'His cousin, Direnç Yilmaz, was convicted of his murder. He'd been paid by a Russian mafia mob to kill another student – a Russian – and you lot decided that he had killed Ekrem as well.'

'And how do you think this is relevant to the death of Professor Hywel Jones?'

'Well…' Gina seemed to falter. 'Well, do you realise that Direnç Yilmaz is Irina Boklova's ex-husband?'

Damn! It came back to her now. Direnç Yilmaz was an obsessively jealous husband. Irina Boklova had come to study in the UK to get away from him. The evidence that he had killed his cousin had been weak, but the prosecution had argued persuasively that he had killed him in a jealous fury.

'So, what are you saying, Gina? That Yilmaz has served his sentence and is here now, posing as a biochemist, still looking out for men who might be interested in his ex-wife? Because I have to tell you that is just about the most absurd idea I have —'

'No.' Gina interrupted, but a bit feebly, Paula thought. 'No, I'm not saying that at all. I –' She stood up. 'I don't know what I meant, actually. I just thought you should be aware of Irina Boklova's history. Criminal connection. But it's nothing really. Wasting your time.' She was moving towards the door. Then she turned. 'I had a long chat with Ruth Curtis,' she said. 'Don't make the mistake of ignoring her as a grieving widow. If she says her husband didn't kill himself, I believe her, and you should too. Good luck with the case.'

And she was out of the door, leaving Paula thinking furiously. Gina had come in intent on telling her something, and she had bottled it, hadn't she? All the stuff about the Yilmaz murder, was that just showing off and wrong-footing her, or was it supposed to lead somewhere? She glanced at Ian Matthews, busily tapping away on his iPad. She ought to discuss this with him but she didn't feel like it: there was too much to explain, and she didn't think he would have anything useful to contribute.

'Ian,' she said, 'ring the station, will you? Get everything you can on the Yilmaz case. I assume that Direnç has done his time. Find out if he was deported afterwards and if not, where he is. I don't think there's anything in this. She's just a woman who likes to think she's cleverer than we are, but it's worth checking.'

He got up to go.

'And see if you can get us some tea, could you?' she said.

She waited until he had closed the door, and then texted Bridget O'Malley: *When you're free can you come here?* Five minutes later, Bridget was at the door.

'I was just going to see if you were free,' she said. 'An interesting development, though I'm not sure if it gets us anywhere.'

'Tell,' Paula said, 'and then I'll tell you mine.'

Bridget O'Malley sat down in the interviewees' chair and said, 'Professor Susan Kessler is an insulin-dependent diabetic.'

'Which might explain why her research group are so protective of her.'

'That's what she said. She gave me a long spiel about how she developed diabetes when she was ten, way back in the late fifties, and the prognosis then wasn't good. There was insulin, but injections were more difficult – and so was blood sugar testing. There was high morbidity – kidney and eye damage, amputations and so on. The doctors told her parents she would be lucky to live to forty.'

'Don't tell me,' Paula said, 'she became a biochemist in order to prove them wrong.'

'Something like that. Her husband worked with her, watched out for her, and established the pattern that her research students were expected to look after her.'

'Which means that they don't just understand how insulin works but they have first-hand knowledge.'

'Exactly.'

'If she told you all this, it sounds as though she was trying to implicate one of them – or to shift suspicion away from herself.'

'Not really,' Bridget O'Malley said. 'We haven't put out the cause of death. There might be speculation, but that's all.'

'Unless she killed him. Then she'd know.'

'Well, of course. But where's the motive?'

Paula shook her head. 'Where's anyone's motive? What have we got? A bit of a spat over some experiments, and a bit of fondling of a female delegate. All in a day's work, you might say. As things stand, my money is still on Hywel Jones himself as having the best motive – the prospect of a long decline, humiliation at the meeting, the opportunity to do it away from his wife's eagle eye.'

'But she says he would never have done it.'

'Maybe that's just her. She was so determined to fight on, he couldn't tell her he didn't have the stomach for it.'

'Maybe,' Bridget said.

They stood and looked at each other.

'What do you want me to do?' Bridget asked.

'See Susan Kessler's research group – especially the women. They had the means – knew how to manage the insulin. I think I should talk to Dr Boklova again. Bloody Gina was going to tell me something about her and then thought better of it. Can you find her – and Dr Alkan – for me?'

Bridget looked stricken. 'They've gone,' she said. 'I saw them getting into a taxi just now. I assumed you had told them they could go.'

'I did. Hell. I'm sure Ian said their flight wasn't till tomorrow.'

'That's suspicious then, isn't it? Taking off like that?'

'It is.'

She called Ian Matthews's number. 'Ian? Did Irina Boklova and her friend sign off with you before they left?'

Ian Matthews sounded defensive. 'They said you'd told them they were free to go.'

'I did, but I didn't mean right away – I meant they could for their flight tomorrow.'

'They said they had an early flight and they were going to stay over at Heathrow.'

'Can you try the airport hotels? Find out if they've booked anywhere?'

'Will do. But can I ask why?'

'You were in the room, Ian. That woman – Gina Gray – didn't you think she was trying to tell us something about them?'

'I didn't think—' he started.

'Just call the hotels, would you?' she said.

'Are we going after them?' Bridget asked.

'I am, DS O'Malley. You are going home to give your kids their tea.'

'You're taking Ian with you?'

'God forbid! Twenty minutes in the car with him coming

from Marlbury was enough for me. I don't need anyone with me. It's an informal chat.'

'You're going all the way to Heathrow for a chat? Are they going to believe that? And if I may say so, boss, you're going to see them because you think they might be killers, so going on your own isn't the best idea.'

'We shall be in a public space. Anyway, there's no-one else available.'

'I'm available. Martin can give the kids their tea. Benefit of having a husband who is a builder. They down tools by four o'clock.'

'I was thinking of meeting up with an officer in the Met,' Paula said. 'Sounds like she's acting SIO on David Scott's attacker.'

'DI?'

'DI Rula Bartosz. Their DCI's on holiday. Or was. He's probably back by now, and she'll be feeling pissed off.'

'And busy, surely?'

'I thought I'd buy her dinner.' She looked at Bridget. 'It's stupid, I know, but he was the best boss I've ever had. I want to see if there's anything I can contribute.'

'I'll call Martin,' Bridget said. 'When do you want to leave?'

Chapter Sixteen

ADHESION

Sunday

By mid-afternoon the optimism of the morning was seeping away, and with it Rula's ability to stay awake. House-to-house inquiries had yielded nothing but bland politeness, and further intensive examination of CCTV footage had produced nothing but headaches and disappointment. If anyone had told Rula that she would be going out for dinner that night, she would have laughed in their face, yet here she was, talking to DI Paula Powell, and hearing herself say, 'Well, in that case, if you're sure, yes.'

She and Paula had never met, but she felt she knew her from working on the Andrew Gray murder with DSu Scott the previous summer. DSu Scott clearly rated her, and Rula had thought, from the tone of their phone conversations in the car, that she probably had a thing for him. The last thing she had expected now, though, was a phone call from her.

It had started badly. Rula, ragged and frustrated, had assumed that, like Gina, Paula Powell was wanting to use her as a channel to privileged information. So she was snappy.

'I can't tell you anything,' she said. 'I've got Gina Gray onto me every five minutes too. We have the same news from

97

the hospital as everyone else – *stable but critical* – and our investigation is going as well as can be expected, given that we have no witnesses, crap CCTV and minimal forensics. Was that what you wanted to know?'

She heard Paula Powell take in a deep breath, like someone about to plunge into icy water. 'I've got to come to London this evening on a case, and I wondered if you wanted to talk,' she said.

'Talk? About DSu Scott?'

'About David, yes.'

'Why? He's not dead, you know.'

'Look, you obviously know much more than I do, but David must have been targeted, mustn't he? It can't have been random. Someone knew he would be running there at that time.'

'We're keeping an open mind. It could have been someone with a grudge against the police – against the Met, maybe.'

'And how would they know he was a police officer?'

'He was outside HQ and heading for the doors.'

'So he could have been a punter – could have been wanting to report a crime.'

Silence. Then Paula Powell said, 'Look, all I'm saying is that David could have been attacked because of something in the past, and I'm part of David's past. I know a few things. Just talking might help.'

Rula felt a great wash of tiredness roll over her. 'I understand that you want to help, but I'm knackered. I need to go home.'

'You need to eat. Look, my interviewees are staying at one of the Hiltons near Heathrow. My DS and I are driving up from Kent now. We can come via Embankment, pick you up and take you to Heathrow. You can have a drink while I'm grilling, and then we'll have dinner and talk. And we'll drop you off home afterwards. Where do you live?'

'Croydon.'

'You remind me why I'm glad I don't work for the Met. But Croydon's hardly out of our way.'

'I'm not dressed for dinner at the Hilton,' Rula objected weakly.

'Nor am I. We'll eat in one of the bars. We've got a couple of things to sort out here, so I'm not sure what time we'll leave, but I'll keep you posted.'

'Paula,' Rula said, 'this interview you're after, is this to do with the professor who died?'

'That was just this morning. How did you hear about it?'

'Gina Gray told me.'

'Of course she did.'

Chapter Seventeen

REFRACTION

Sunday

All right. I admit it. I failed. When it came to the crunch, I was a coward. I bottled it, chickened out, backed down, backed off and backpedalled, cried off and wimped out, funked it and flunked it, reneged and abnegated. Worse than that, I have probably sent Paula off on a fool's errand, a wild goose chase and a lost cause, looking for Direnç Yilmaz, who emerged as a suspect from my pathetic attempt to put Irina in the frame without confessing to my secret knowledge and buried crime.

I am a moral coward, Immanuel Kant would despise me, and my only excuse is that today is one of the worst days of my life and it is very unkind of anyone to expect me to be perfect.

Chapter Eighteen

FACILITATED DIFFUSION

'Well, I'm telling you now.'

Freda lay on her bed and let her mother's complaints wash over her. She should have told her before about what had happened, she knew, but it was exactly this – this fretting and fussing and blaming – that had made her find excuses for delaying. And she had been busy. Really. Faith and Lisa had both left, so she was the only help Alice had. This break, before it was time to set up for dinner, was the first proper one she had had.

Suddenly she snapped alert to what her mother was saying.

'...right away,' she heard. 'He'll be with you in half an hour. Make sure you're packed and ready.'

'Mum, no!' she protested. 'What do you mean?'

'Ben's coming to bring you home.'

'Mum, I can't. Lisa and Faith have gone home. I said I'd stay and help Alice with supper, and breakfast tomorrow. I'll get the train in the morning and go straight to school, like we agreed.'

'You will not, Freda. What are you thinking? Why do you think the other girls' parents have taken them home?'

'Well, it was Faith's stepdad who died, so it's not surprising if—'

'They've taken them home because it's not safe there. And if you'd let us know sooner, we'd—'

'It's perfectly safe here, Mum. Most likely Hywel Jones died accidentally. It's not like there's a murderer stalking the corridors.'

'You said the police were there.'

'Only because it's a sudden death. It's just standard practice.'

'I know you, Freda. There's some sort of mystery about his death, and you think you can solve it. The only thing to be grateful for is that you haven't got Granny there.'

What a good thing it was that people couldn't see you blushing over the phone, Freda thought. She said, 'She's got other things to worry about.'

'And that's another thing,' her mother said, now in full hyper-anxiety mode. 'Do you know where she is? There's no reply from her landline, and all I get from her mobile are text messages that tell me nothing. I've rung Annie, but she's only had texts too. Have you heard from her?'

'Well… you know… texts…' Freda squirmed. Why was she so bad at this? Better to change the subject. 'Look, Mum, I'll try and find out how many people are staying for dinner, and how many are staying over. I might be able to come home after we've cleared dinner.'

'I think I'd better talk to this woman Alice.'

'I'll do it, Mum. Alice hasn't had an easy day any more than the rest of us. She doesn't need hassle from you.'

'Well, do it then. You're not sleeping another night in that place,' her mother said. 'I don't care how many people don't get their breakfast.'

She rang off while Freda was still opening her mouth to reply.

Freda sat up. She was conscious of feeling something unexpected and recognised it, after a moment, as relief.

102

She looked across at Faith's bed, already stripped, with the sheets in a neat bundle on the end of it, and she thought of that morning, waking to the light from Faith's laptop screen and then hearing Lisa's running feet and the pounding on the door. If she slept here, those would be the images that swarmed through her dreams, she knew. They might be there anyway, but at least at home she would open her eyes to what was safe and familiar, go downstairs and make cocoa, know that Mum and Ben and Nico were there, that all the people she loved were safe. Except for Granny. If she left here, what would Granny do?

Chapter Nineteen

ACTIVE TRANSPORT

Sunday

Paula Powell, Bridget O'Malley and Rula Bartosz stood in the foyer of the Hilton hotel and Paula wondered if anyone would have guessed that they were police officers. It wouldn't have been difficult to rule out sun and surf as their airborne destination, so anyone who bothered to wonder would have assumed that they were on some sort of work trip, but police? She didn't think so.

She looked around, slightly dazed by bright lights, chrome surfaces, and a clattering hubbub hardly muffled by miles of angrily patterned carpet. She looked at Rula, who looked greenish grey in the unforgiving fluorescence.

'I'm thinking a change of plan,' she said. 'My idea was to leave you in the bar while Bridget and I talk to Dr Boklova, and then we'd all have dinner, but I don't think you're safe to be left alone. One drink and you'll be flat out.'

'I'm all right.'

'I think we'll take you with us. Three of us just might rattle Dr Boklova's cage – especially if I tell her you're from the Met.'

'It's not my case. I don't know the details.'

'You don't have to say anything. Just look enigmatic.'

The look on Irina Boklova's face when she opened the door of her hotel room told Paula that her gamble had paid off. The woman was rattled. She soon covered it, of course, but Paula had seen fear as well as surprise. Ceren Alkan was slower to recover, looking as though she would like to burrow into the sofa she was sitting on. But then she had been as jumpy as a cat in a thunderstorm even in the innocuous interview they had had earlier. What did they know? This was her last throw at finding out.

Even though the room was some sort of deluxe super room – the kind Paula automatically ignored when booking holidays online – Paula and her colleagues managed to fill it, demolishing what had been set up as a scene of domestic tranquillity. The two women were wearing the hotel's fluffy, white dressing gowns, their hair wet from the shower. On a coffee table lay the remains of a room service supper, including a bottle in an ice bucket. A joss stick was burning in a saucer.

'Sorry to disturb your evening,' Paula said, taking no trouble to sound sincere. 'Let me introduce my colleagues. Detective Sergeant Bridget O'Malley from the Kent police force, and Detective Inspector Rula Bartosz, representing the Metropolitan police.'

Irina Boklova was as rattled by mention of the Met as Paula had hoped.

'Why the Metropolitan police?' she asked. 'And why another interview? We both answered your questions this afternoon.'

'You did,' Paula said, settling herself on a sofa facing the one on which Ceren Alkan was huddled, and where Irina Boklova had joined her. Bridget O'Malley sat beside Paula, and Rula sat herself on the only other seat in the room – a wheeled office chair by a large pine desk.

'You answered my questions,' Paula said, 'but you withheld information that could be very helpful to our investigation. Why did you do that?'

She let her eyes dwell on Ceren Alkan, but it was Irina Boklova who answered.

'We have no idea what you are talking about.'

Paula leant forward. 'Why did you come to the conference in Stourly?' she asked. 'Both of you?'

'I was invited to give a paper. And Dr Alkan's research is in a relevant discipline.'

'But you both know the area well, don't you? You were students in Marlbury. Are you telling me that your decision to come had nothing to do with coming back for old times' sake?'

Irina Boklova took a swig from her wine glass and laughed. 'Full marks for looking up our police records, Inspector, but didn't they tell you that our time in Kent wasn't exactly a happy one?'

'When did you last see Direnç Yilmaz?' Paula asked, and saw Irina Bokova's mouth drop open.

'What?'

'When did you last see your husband, Direnç Yilmaz?'

'My ex-husband, you mean. I have remarried.' She took hold of Ceren Alkan's hand. 'I last saw Direnç more than fifteen years ago, before he committed murder. I didn't go to his trial.'

'He was released from prison two years ago.'

'By which time I had divorced him and remarried. I have no idea where he is.'

'Your husband was obsessed with you. You came to the UK to study in order to get away from him, but he followed you, and murdered his cousin because he believed you were having an affair with him. He was deported back to Turkey when he was released. It wouldn't have been easy for him to get to you in the US, but here, with his criminal connections and our porous sea coasts, it would be easy for him to get into Kent, wouldn't it?'

'To find me?' Irina Boklova was overacting her incredulity, Paula thought. 'Even if he wanted, how would he know where I was?'

'Oh, come on, Dr Boklova. He only had to put your name into a search engine, and there you would be, speaking at a conference at Stourly College, programme, dates and times helpfully provided.'

Silence. Irina Boklova refilled her glass. Then she leant forward and fixed Paula with her pale blue gaze.

'You're investigating Professor Hywel Jones's death. (Which, by the way, we all think was suicide. The man had just been diagnosed with Alzheimer's.) But just supposing my ex-husband tracked me down to Stourly College and risked drowning to come and find me, how come, in your scenario, he ended up killing Hywel Jones? How does that work exactly?'

Paula felt herself beginning to sweat. She knew who this woman reminded her of. It was Martina Navratilova, and it was going to be game, set and match in the blink of an eye. She cleared her throat.

'It seems Professor Jones had wandering hands.' She looked at Ceren Alkan. 'Dr Alkan can testify to that. And we have a witness who says that you saw the harassment of Dr Alkan yesterday and you looked furious. Was that because you had suffered the same treatment from him? If so – and if your pathologically jealous ex-husband knew about it – that's a motive, isn't it? Just as it was his motive for killing his cousin.'

Irina Boklova threw back her head and gave what sounded like a genuine bellow of laughter. She put down her glass in order to tick off her objections.

'First, I am quite a famous lesbian, you know, so Hywel was unlikely to try his luck with me. Second, Direnç would have had to see him with me. How do you imagine he was watching me? Hiding in plain sight?'

'If it's more than fifteen years since you saw him, he will have changed. Prison changes people, for a start.'

'OK. So he has plastic surgery, he shaves his head, he grows a beard. How does he get to register for a specialist scientific conference? Where are his credentials?'

'He worked for a Russian mafia boss. That would be child's play.'

'And how does he convince when he's with the other delegates? Talking biochemistry?'

Paula smiled. She had been storing up the information that Ian Matthews had sent her when she was in the car.

'How did you meet your husband, Dr Boklova?'

Irina Boklova looked wary. 'I was on holiday on the Black Sea coast, and so was he, staying in the same resort.'

'And you found that you had things in common, didn't you? You were a medical student and he had just qualified as a doctor.'

Irina Boklova shrugged. 'He was not serious. He had no dedication.'

'He certainly didn't. You married, he went to Russia with you and got a job in a Moscow hospital, but he soon found that stealing and selling drugs suited him better than treating patients. So he was never much of a doctor, but I guess he would have remembered enough to talk the talk at the conference. Anyway, someone who keeps quiet and listens makes themself very popular. People would much rather talk than be talked at.'

Irina Boklova drained her glass, seemed to consider refilling it and decided against it. She leant back on her sofa. 'It's a nice little story you're telling yourself, Inspector, but you still can't give me a reason why Direnç would kill Hywel Jones. Jealousy about me really won't play. If he was watching me then it would be Ceren he would go after.' She took her partner's hand again. 'She is my wife, after all. She replaced him.'

Paula had one possible answer to this – a flimsy one, and Irina Boklova was probably about to blow it away.

'At the end of the conference session where your paper had triggered the big row, what did you do?'

Irina Boklova looked at her wife. 'We had tea, didn't we? Well, coffee actually – neither of us can stand tea. And we talked with people about my paper. There was quite a lot that people wanted to discuss, and the discussion had been derailed by the row.'

'But Hywel Jones left. Did anyone go after him?'

'I don't know. I don't think so. He looked pretty toxic. He needed to cool off.'

'What about later? It seems no-one remembers him being at dinner.'

'He wasn't. I went to his room after dinner. I guess I felt somewhat responsible – it was my paper that led to his – I don't know – shaming, I guess.'

'You didn't mention this earlier.'

'He wasn't there. I knocked twice.'

'Did you go in?'

'Why would I?'

'But you could have been seen going to his room.'

'Don't you think I would have noticed if my ex-husband had been following me down the corridors?'

Paula stood up. 'Before we let you go on your way back to the US,' she said, 'I'd like DS O'Malley to take a look at your phone. You say you have had no contact with your ex-husband, but I would like to check whether he has tried to make contact with you. There is a good deal of information about you on the University of Berkely website. He could certainly have your email, and it wouldn't have been difficult for him to get hold of your phone number.'

'I don't answer unfamiliar numbers.'

'Exactly. And you probably have a strong spam filter on your emails. I'd like to take a look.'

'And if I don't give you my phone?'

'Then I'll have to take your passports – yours and Dr Alkan's – and apply for warrants and so-on. It could take a while.'

'How long will you need it for?'

Paula looked at Bridget. 'A couple of hours?'

Silently, Irina Boklova reached into the pocket of her bathrobe and handed over her phone.

Chapter Twenty

AFFINITY

Sunday

Outside the hotel room, Rula followed Paula and Bridget down a corridor. The thick carpet felt treacherous under her feet and her head felt somehow full of air. She was quite likely to fall down, she thought. Lack of sleep and, possibly, food. When had she last eaten anything? And before she fell down she needed to tell Paula something. She had had an idea, while Paula was talking to Irina Boklova, but it was getting away from her.

Paula turned round and called over her shoulder, 'I'm going to see if I can book us a room for a couple of hours. We'll order room service and Bridget can work on the phone.'

'Can you do that? Just for a couple of hours?'

'Watch me.'

Rula followed, along corridors and down stairs, and then, in the vast foyer, in sight of the reception desk, Bridget O'Malley stopped. 'You go ahead,' she said to Paula. 'We'll wait for you here.'

'It's all right,' Paula said. 'I'm not going to make a scene. I'm sure you can book a room by the hour in a place like this.'

'It's not that.' Bridget's face was turning scarlet. 'It's not that. It's just the three of us, you know, wanting a room…'

Paula gave a hoot of laughter. 'A kinky threesome! They'll think we want a kinky threesome?'

'Well,' Bridget mumbled. 'You know…'

'And paid for with public money! *Police officers in luxury hotel sex party!*'

'If you worked for the Met, you wouldn't joke,' Rula said. 'It's just the sort of story the media would love at the moment.'

'We'll record ourselves. I want Rula's take on Boklova and Alkan, and I want to hear about progress with finding David's killer. And you, Bridget, are going to be reporting on the contents of that phone. So, as soon as we get into the room, I'll set my phone to record. But you can wait here while I make the booking – just to spare your blushes, Bridget.'

She marched off, and Rula moved to lean against a wall.

'Are you all right?' Bridget asked.

Rula liked her accent – the way she said *orl roight*. 'Can I tell you something?' she asked. 'I had an idea while we were in there, but I'm so tired, I think I might forget it before I have a chance to tell Paula.'

'We can find you a chair.' She looked around. 'There must be one somewhere.'

'No, it's all right. It's just – I think there could be a connection between the two cases.'

'Which two?'

'Your murder in Kent and the attack on David Scott.'

Bridget O'Malley smiled. 'That would be a bit of a wild coincidence, wouldn't it?'

'I know. But I had it all clear in my mind before.' She slid down the wall that was propping her up, and sat with her head on her knees. 'It's about the boat,' she said.

Paula returned, waving a key card, and between them she and Bridget hauled Rula to her feet and propelled her into a lift and down more corridors. In their room, she slumped gratefully onto the large bed, heedless of the tastefully arranged cushions. 'Just resting for five minutes,' she mumbled.

From her prone position she heard Paula and Rula surveying the room.

'Not *deluxe*, nor even *superior*,' Paula said, 'but the budget goes only so far. It's got what we need. There's a desk there for you, and look – a room service menu.' Then Rula heard her hoot with delight. 'We can have chicken and chips in a basket! How retro is that? My parents used sometimes to take my brother and me to a pub with a garden for Sunday lunch, and I always had chicken in a basket.'

'I don't think pubs had gardens where I grew up,' Bridget said.

'Oh sorry, Bridget. I forgot you grew up on the mean streets of Brum, and your father was only a humble headmaster!'

'Order me the chicken and I can feel posh!'

Paula came over to the bed. 'How about you, Rula?' she asked.

'Whatever,' she mumbled.

'I'd love a glass of wine, but you're driving, Bridget, and Rula's half asleep as it is, so mineral water and coffee all round, I suppose,' Paula said, and Rula heard her pick up the phone and ring with their order.

'Were you serious about recording us?' Bridget asked.

'I think it's not a bad idea. I'm hoping when Rula's had something to eat she'll have some ideas about our case.'

'She has. Something about a boat, wasn't it, Rula?'

'Okay,' Paula said. 'Don't know what that's about but I'm starting recording now.'

The chips were delicious – hot, crisp and meltingly soft inside – and the chicken was good too – Rula was sure there

113

was a hint of paprika there, rubbed into the glossy brown skin. She could feel the food reviving her, could almost monitor the rise in her blood sugar. Seeing that Paula and Bridget were taking their time, talking while eating, occasionally waving a chip around as they got animated, she slowed herself down after the first ravenous mouthfuls and concentrated on savouring the food. The other two were talking shop, Paula defending her pursuit of Direnç Yilmaz as prime suspect, while Bridget was sceptical.

'I think Irina Boklova's got a point. How does an outsider gatecrash a scientific meeting and get away with it? OK, he was a doctor years ago so he might know a bit of the jargon, but he'd have to have an affiliation. They all wear name badges with their university or whatever, don't they?'

'He works for a Russian mafia boss – or did. Even if he's lost his old job, he'll still know people. Fake ID would be no problem.'

'Even so, it'd need to be a real place, and then someone says, *Oh I see you work at x – you must know my good friend so-and-so* et cetera, et cetera.'

'Well, have you got a better suggestion? We're looking for a murderer. You know as well as I do that the majority of murders in this country are committed by people who are already operating in the criminal world. Irina Boklova's link to Yilmaz is the only whiff of a criminal connection we have found so far. You couldn't find a more harmless lot of herbivores than the attendees at that conference.'

'What about the guy who had the row with Hywel Jones at the meeting and stormed out? We haven't talked to him, have we?'

'Only because we agreed to see the people with flights to catch first. He's on my list for first thing tomorrow.'

'OK. We'll see then. And in the meantime I'll look at this phone. There's a limit to what I can do here, but I'll do my best.'

She got up and went over to the desk, where she switched on a lamp and settled down.

'Coffee?' Paula asked.

'Please.'

Paula poured three cups of coffee from a thermos jug, took one to Bridget and pushed one over to Rula.

'So,' she said, 'what's this about a boat?'

For a moment, Rula felt panicky. The fog was clearing from her brain, but clarity only made her wonder if she was just being absurd.

'You'll probably think this is nonsense,' she said.

'Bridget thinks my scenario is nonsense. Try me.'

Rula took a swig of coffee. 'It was when you talked about Yilmaz possibly coming here on one of the channel boats. It rang a bell because the only smidgeon of a clue that we have about David's attacker is a couple who got off the first train from Dover early on Saturday morning.'

'A couple?'

'A man and a young girl. A ticket collector was suspicious about them – thought she might be being coerced. And she could be the same girl – or young woman – we have on CCTV on the Embankment at the time of the attack. There's a man with her, but his face isn't visible. We think he may have known where the cameras are.'

'So what's your story?'

'We've got David on CCTV, finishing his run and starting to cross the road to go into HQ. Then he turns and crosses back again – and then goes out of range.'

'So something happened to make him turn back.'

'We think so. We have some foreign DNA taken from David. There's male skin and traces of female blood.'

'So he was being a hero? Going to help the girl?'

'It's a possibility. And it's a possibility that it was a set-up – to lure him over. It's pretty fragile, but it's all we've got.'

'OK. So this links to Hywel Jones how?'

'Well, you're thinking that Yilmaz could have come back because he was still obsessed with his ex-wife, but David led the investigation that ended with him being sent to jail. Suppose he saw the chance to get revenge on him?' She leant forward, completely awake now. 'Like you say, he gets a boat over here. He's got the right connections to get into something that is actually a functioning boat, and he does a bit of trafficking on the side. Maybe he's doing it to earn his passage, maybe it's a bit of private enterprise on his part. Either way, he has a girl in tow, and he's delivering her to a nail bar or a "hotel" or whatever, and it's near Met HQ, which gives him a kick. And then he hits the jackpot. Who should come running along, all alone in the early morning, but the man who sent him to jail. He carries a knife with him as a matter of course. All he has to do is scare the girl, so she cries out, and David does his Sir Galahad act, and there we are.'

'Then he drops the girl off and heads back down to Kent?'

'Yes.'

'The ticket collector. What description did he give of the man he saw?'

'In his thirties, dark, clean shaven, hair hidden by a beanie.'

'I checked out Yilmaz's mugshot from when he was arrested. That's fifteen years old, of course. He's dark and hairy.'

'So the beanie would be a useful disguise.'

'But why would he target Hywel Jones? Like Irina said, it's Ceren Alkan he should be jealous of.'

'I've thought about that. I think a man like that, with his background, could well not have realised what their relationship is. I'll bet women don't come out as lesbian in Turkey – or Russia. And think what it would do to his pride to think that a woman who has been married to him would actually prefer to have sex with a woman.'

'OK, but why Hywel Jones?'

'Did you notice what Irina Boklova said when you asked her if she went into his room when she went looking for him?'

'She said she didn't.'

'That wasn't what she said, actually. What she said was *Why would I?* That's what you say to avoid a direct lie. If she knocked on his door and got no reply, wouldn't she have tried the door? She was there because she was worried about him. She wouldn't just go away. And if she tried the door and it wasn't locked, she would have gone in to check that he was all right.'

'So why didn't she say so?'

'I'd guess because she stayed and had a snoop around and she didn't want to say so.'

'Why snoop? What would she have been looking for?'

'People just snoop. I heard the results of a survey once. People were asked if they would look into the bathroom cabinet in someone else's house. Eighty per cent of the sample said that they sometimes or *always* looked. People are just nosey.'

'If she looked in his en suite, she'll have found his insulin.'

'True. But she's not a suspect, is she?'

'No. Though I have this niggling feeling that Gina Gray was wanting to tell me something about her but changed her mind.'

'The point about her looking round the room is that Yilmaz might have seen her go into the room and stay there. To him that could suggest that they were on familiar terms.'

'It's pretty thin as a motive. It's not as though she would have been in there long enough for him to think that they were having sex. And there's another problem. Jealousy can be a motive for murder, but the killer wants his/her victim to know they're being punished. The point about Hywel Jones's death was that he was injected while he was asleep, so he knew nothing about it. And the killer hoped it would pass as accident or suicide. It looks much more like a killing by someone who just wanted him out of the way.'

'That would be because he knew something, wouldn't it?'

'Most likely.'

Paula leant back in her chair. 'It's just all too flimsy, isn't it?' she said. 'We can't run with it.'

And then Bridget scooted back the office chair she was sitting in, and spun it round to face them. 'Don't speak too soon,' she said. 'Help is at hand.' She brandished Irina Boklova's phone. 'I've only looked back over calls in the last month so far. But in that time there have been five calls from a foreign mobile number. The number is not in her contacts, and all the calls have gone unanswered. I checked the country of registration for that number, and it is guess what?

'Not Turkey?' Rula asked.

'Bingo!' Bridget answered.

'Blimey,' Paula said.

Chapter Twenty-One

SILENT MUTATION

Monday

So this is how things stand. It is three minutes past ten on Monday morning, fifty-one hours since David was attacked. I have gone through the absurd password business with the hospital, only to be told that David had another *comfortable night*. This time I didn't challenge the evidential basis for this. They have broken my spirit. I did raise, hopelessly, the question of my visiting him, and was given no encouragement. The implication is that my very presence in his room could finish him off.

I have rung Alessandro to find out whether representatives of the Fourth Estate are still camped at my door. He tells me that they have taken themselves off, leaving an *'orrible mess* behind them (Italians, like French speakers, have trouble with our initial aspirates). The place is littered with cigarette butts, paper coffee cups and beer cans, he tells me, but when his sons get back from school he will send them round to clear up. He and his family – a quiet, beautiful wife and two smiling, bright-eyed boys – live above the restaurant, and the boys are old enough now to be drafted in for washing up when things get busy.

'I'll pay them when I get back,' I say.

'They will do it for a bowl of tartufo *al Ciocolato*,' he says.

When I get back, I told him, because there is no reason now for me to stay here, is there? Except that I don't want to go back, because that will mean returning to normal life, and I need to maintain my vigil. Because this immuring of myself is somewhere between vigil and penance. Given the grudging hospitality here, it is quite easy to make it a penance. My only breakfast this morning was a cup of tea. I learnt enough yesterday not to risk the unspeakable coffee again, and the dining room so reeked of burnt toast and ancient fry-ups that I couldn't face eating. Later I will go and eat something at the café. No more cake. Yesterday I had Ruth Curtis as my excuse; today I eat only because starving myself will be no help.

Today will be more of a penance because Freda has gone, and there is nothing to watch from my window. I saw Ben arrive and carry Freda off yesterday evening, and this morning I watched while the conference attendees who didn't get away yesterday make their escape. There has been no sign of Paula, or any of her sidekicks.

Of course, I am not without entertainment. I have my phone, which offers me the world – communication written and oral, twenty-four-hour news, the information highway, music, audiobooks, and games, games, games. There is a rather good non-crime novel by Agatha Christie, writing as Mary Westmacott. It is called, I think, *Absent in the Spring*. In it, a middle-aged Englishwoman is returning home, by train, from a visit to her married daughter, living in Iraq. Her journey is disrupted by floods, which cause landslides and block the railway lines, and she finds herself alone for several days in a 'rest house' next to a station in the desert. The only other person there is the local man who manages the rest house and cooks basic meals (mainly eggs, as I recall) and speaks only basic English. Once the woman has finished the only book she has with her, and has used up her small stock of writing paper and the ink in her fountain pen, she has absolutely nothing to occupy her. Even going for a walk is impossible because there are no landmarks in the surrounding desert, and she quickly gets disoriented. And so the point of the book is that this woman, who has always been, we realise, a self-satisfied busybody, is forced to sit and consider her life, and to confront the realisation that she has been neither as good nor as successful as she has believed herself to be. It is very well done, with a nice sting in the tail, and Christie herself said that it was her only book that truly satisfied her. This is a long diversion, and you may wonder what my point is, but I suppose that I am making the fairly banal observation that we think our phones keep us connected to the real world, but actually, most of the time, we use them to distract ourselves from the real world – in particular from the very real and very terrifying world inside our heads. All right, this is not original. I am not at my best. What do you want from me?

Remembering Christie's heroine and her diet of eggs makes me decide to go out to my café. I will order a poached egg on toast. I find eggs rather disgusting, so it will make a good penance.

Chapter Twenty-Two

ANTIBODIES

Monday

Freda didn't know quite what an out-of-body experience was, but she was fairly sure she was having one. She thought she had negotiated the return to school pretty well, fending off eager enquiries with polite casualness, but when Mr Murray asked her how far she thought George Eliot invited the reader to sympathise with Rosamonde Viney, she looked blankly at her copy of *Middlemarch*, open in front of her, and had no idea what he was talking about. At the end of the lesson, Mr Murray held her back and asked her if she was all right, and Freda gave him a cheery smile and said she was fine – just a bit short of sleep – before heading for the loos and shutting herself in a cubicle until she felt she could face the common room. Her mum had wanted her to take the day off. Lisa's mother had rung her, and said she was keeping Lisa at home, but Freda had insisted on going in. Being on her own at home would have been worse. She had seen Faith briefly, going into assembly with her friends forming a sort of bodyguard around her. She looked pale, and gave Freda the briefest of smiles.

At the end of the morning, having struggled to concentrate through a psychology lesson, she found Mrs Mancini, the head of pastoral care, waiting outside the classroom. 'I thought we should have a chat,' she said. 'Mr Murray was worried about you.'

So, instead of eating her pitta and hummus, which Ben had kindly packed for her, she found herself with tea and cake in Mrs Mancini's untidy little office. Mrs M would get on well with Granny, she thought, with their shared belief in the curative properties of cake. But Mrs M was doing her best, so Freda was polite. She didn't mention David, with his life hanging by a thread, nor her grandmother, looking old and lost. She ate her cake, again excused her lapse over *Middlemarch* on the grounds of shortage of sleep, and explained that of course the experience over the weekend had not been as bad for her as it had been for Faith, or indeed for Lisa, who had actually found Professor Jones.

'So, really, I'm fine,' she said, and then, horrifyingly, she felt a huge, unstoppable sob rise up in her chest, and she heard herself give an odd, strangled wail before bursting into tears.

Mrs Mancini was kind, of course, as Freda sobbed and apologised and mopped herself up with a handful of tissues from the monster pack that the head of pastoral care kept on her desk.

'You need to be kind to yourself, Freda,' she said, once the storm of weeping had subsided. 'You had a shock. You coped with it very well. You were the one who called 999, weren't you? But you saw a dead body, and not many sixteen-year-olds have done that – in this country, anyway.'

Freda sniffed and nodded. 'I guess,' she said, but even as she said it, she knew that it wasn't delayed shock that was getting to her – or not altogether, anyway. The thing that was making her feel sick and wobbly and panicky was that she had seen something. She knew she had seen something yesterday morning, and she thought it was the answer, but her mind refused to tell her what it was.

123

Chapter Twenty-Three

ELIMINATION

Monday

At 9.15 in the morning Paula received a text from Rula. It seemed no time since they had dropped Rula at her flat in Croydon, and driven back to Kent, so when she saw Rula's name on a new text, she assumed it was just a *thanks for the lift and the chat* message, but not so. Rula was right back in work mode and Paula had to snap in too.

RULA   *Bad news on Yilmaz DNA. No match with DNA on David. So much for a good theory. How about your end?*

PAULA   *Bummer! Was relying on you. No poss perp DNA at our scene. Assume gloves.*

RULA   *Planned then?*

PAULA   *Seems so but scientists use gloves all the time.*

RULA   *At a meeting? Do drs take their stethoscopes?*

PAULA   *OK but planning knocks the jealousy scenario.*

RULA   *Yeah xx*

Paula put her phone away and realised that she was smiling.

It was hardly good news that forensics didn't bear out Rula's theory about Direnç Yilmaz; the smile was for those two *x*s.

Her good mood evaporated as her phone rang again. It was Bridget O'Malley this time, sounding very unlike her usual competent self.

'I'm sorry,' she said. 'Bit of a crisis here. I think Martin has broken his foot. Silly sod played football with the boys yesterday and tripped and fell awkwardly. He's been in agony all night. Hasn't slept, so I haven't either, of course. I'm getting the blame 'cos I wasn't here so he couldn't leave the kids and go to A&E, though actually Maggie next door would have kept an eye on them. Anyway, I need to drive him to the hospital now, so I'll be late in, I'm afraid. And I'll need to pick the kids up from school. He's not going to be able to drive with that foot. I'll get something sorted for the rest of the week but—'

'Bridget!' Paula said. 'Stop. Slow down. Take the day off. You'll be most of the morning in A&E anyway, and you haven't had any sleep so you won't be much use. Stay at home with Martin, give him some TLC, pick the kids up, have an early night. You did hours of overtime yesterday, anyway, driving to Heathrow and back.'

'Are you sure?'

Paula could feel the relief. 'Absolutely sure. I shall take young Ian to the uni with me to interview the snotty guy who had a tantrum at Hywel Jones's lecture. He'll like that.'

She went down to the incident room which had been set up on the ground floor, and found Ian Matthews at a computer screen, unenthusiastically scanning a series of faces.

'What have you got there?' she asked.

'Hywel Jones's secretary has sent copies of the registration details for the conference delegates. We ran names through the system yesterday and drew a blank – all clean as whistles except for Dr Irina Boklova, and that's her ex-husband, not her. But I thought I'd try running their mugshots just in case.'

'Good thinking. Anything?'

'Not so far.'

'Do you want to take a break and come with me to the uni to interview Hywel Jones's postdoc?'

'Yes, please.' He jumped up and picked up his leather jacket from the back of his chair.

As they walked to the car, he said, 'Remind me what a postdoc is.'

'He's got his PhD but he's not got a lectureship. He's working in Hywel Jones's research group.'

'Not any more.'

'What do you mean?'

'Well, presumably the research group is defunct along with Hywel Jones.'

'How elegantly you express things. Yes, I suppose so. Which casts some doubt on his having a motive for killing Hywel Jones.'

'So why are we talking to him?'

'He seems to have had an altercation with Hywel Jones on Saturday afternoon. Jones gave a lecture – a research paper – and was challenged about his research findings. It seems that Jones blamed his postdoc – Dr Crawley – and Crawley stormed out.'

In the car, as they were driving up the hill to the university, Paula said, 'The interesting thing is that it was the girl who was serving tea at the conference session who told me about the blow-up between Hywel Jones and Dr Crawley. None of the academics mentioned it, which is odd.'

'Maybe these rows happen all the time and they thought nothing of it.'

'Maybe. And teenage girls love a drama. It's like catnip to them.'

'Did she say anything about him – Crawley?'

'She couldn't remember his name but said it was something posh. I got his name from Professor Pratt.'

'Crawley? Posh?' He laughed. 'Have you ever been to Crawley?'

'I have, but it wasn't that Crawley she was thinking of. I'm guessing she was thinking of *Downton*.'

'*Downton*?'

'*Downton Abbey*. The earl's family are called Crawley, aren't they?'

'I wouldn't know. My mum used to watch it.'

Of course she did, Paula thought. Everywhere in this country there were men saying, *My mum/wife/girlfriend watches/reads that*, as though having a woman do it for them relieved them of the burden of tangling with fiction – too messy, too emotional, too complicated. Not that anyone was missing out by not watching *Downton*, she thought. She had given up on it herself in the first or second episode, when the Turk died in Lady Mary's bed, and it was too preposterous to be fun, but lockdown had forced her to watch the repeats – you had to lower your standards and find your comfort where you could. It was like eating chocolate.

She said, 'Freda Gray said Dr Crawley sounded posh – reminded her of the boys at the Abbey School.'

'I'm going to love him then,' he said. 'Just my kind of guy.'

And Paula thought that antagonism was just what she had brought him for. He might get under the other man's skin. She said, 'I had to put the gag on you yesterday because I needed to get through those interviews fast, but feel free to chip in with Crawley.'

'Right,' he said. 'Thanks.'

The signage on the campus was unhelpful, abandoning them once they found the Science Park, but they located the Biochemistry building eventually, and then Hywel Jones's lab. Dr Alaric Crawley (really, some parents didn't make life easy for their kids) met them there and took them to what he called *a quiet spot*, but which looked to Paula more like a store cupboard. He was a slight young man with short, mousey hair and steel-rimmed glasses, but he managed an air of authority all the same, and took charge, bringing in folding chairs and offering coffee from a machine in the corner. *Establishing his role as helpful witness*, Paula thought. *No question of his being a suspect.* She sniffed the air, taking in the quasi-medical tang. This young man was also making them the outsiders in his home territory. They would need to make him uncomfortable, and DC Matthews seemed to be on it right away.

'So,' he said, while they were still organising their chairs in the small space, 'you've lost your boss. How do you feel about that?'

Alaric Crawley stiffened. '*Boss* isn't really a term we use in academia,' he said.

'No? What would you call him then?'

'He was the grant-holder for our research.'

'Grant-holder?'

'He had charge of our funding.'

'And that funding is from the university?'

Alaric Crawley laughed. 'Oh no. The university doesn't have that sort of money. We academics have to bring in funding.'

'So where does your funding come from?'

'From the ARC – the Agriculture Research Council.'

'That sounds like public money – our money.'

'If you like.'

'I don't have a choice, do I?'

'I meant—'

'And Professor Jones paid you out of that money?'

'Yes.'

'Well, in my world that makes him your boss.'

'Academic work is collegial. We eschew hierarchies.'

Paula decided it was time to intervene.

'And did you get on, collegially, with Professor Jones, Dr Crawley?'

'For the most part.'

'And the other part?'

'There are always disagreements about approaches and priorities.'

'Of course. Tell me about the disagreement on Saturday afternoon.'

Crawley sat back in his chair in what looked like a conscious effort to appear relaxed. 'Dr Boklova's paper raised some quite fundamental issues, and there was a lively discussion after it.'

'And what were those issues?'

'It would be difficult to explain to a layman – or laywoman,' he said. And then he smirked. It was definitely a smirk, Paula decided.

'This laywoman has a chemistry degree,' she said. 'Try me.'

He flushed slightly but continued to lounge. 'Nutritional advantage,' he said. 'The evidence for the comparative nutritional value of GM and non-GM crops is partial and somewhat contradictory at the moment. Dr Boklova presented her findings that the GM crops she studied offered no additional nutritional value.'

'And in the course of lively *discussion* that followed her paper, you stormed out of the conference room.'

Now he sat up straight. 'I left the room. I didn't *storm out*.'

'That was the word that our witness used. Can you tell us what upset you so much?'

Alaric Crawley's mouth twisted in distaste. '*Upset* is hardly the word I would use. I was – quite justifiably – angry.'

'Tell us about it.'

'I really don't see how this can have any relevance to—'

Paula cut him off. 'Professor Jones's death is, at the moment, unexplained. We know how he died but we don't know why, and we owe it to his family to establish that. What happened to him in the hours before his death is crucial to our inquiry. So tell us, please, Dr Crawley, why you were angry and what exactly happened in the altercation that ended with you leaving the conference room.'

Instead of answering, Crawley got up and went to stand at the room's very small window. As far as Paula could see, there was no view except of the wall of an adjoining building, but Crawley stood gazing out before turning back to them and saying, 'You think he killed himself, and you think I'm responsible.'

It wasn't a question. Paula didn't bother with the *we're pursuing several possible lines of inquiry* get-out. She said, 'Are you telling me that hasn't already crossed your mind?'

Crawley came back to his seat, but sat on the edge of it, leaning forward, hands on knees. 'Look,' he said, 'Hywel – Professor Jones – wasn't an easy man to work with – especially not in the last few months. He had fixed ideas and wasn't readily open to discussion. He was pleased with some of the results we had, and he wrote them up in a paper for one of our professional journals. I didn't' think we were ready for that – there were some more experiments we needed to do to make our findings watertight – but Hywel was in a hurry and said we could do those later. I realise now, knowing about his Alzheimer's diagnosis, why he was in a hurry – he knew that he had little productive work time left – but at the time I was annoyed about it. Anyway, I was proved right. When the paper was sent out for peer review, the referees sent it back with the recommendation that those very experiments that I wanted to do should be done and included in the paper before it could be regarded as publishable. I was vindicated, and I expected then to go ahead with the further work.'

'But you didn't?' Paula asked.

'No!' Crawley was more relaxed now, confident in the rightness of his own case. 'Hywel dismissed the recommendations of the referees, and said he would try the paper with some other journals.'

'So what did you do?'

'There was nothing I could do, except do the work behind his back, but that wasn't possible because it required some expensive equipment, which Hywel would have to authorise.'

'Because he was boss,' Ian Matthews murmured.

Paula said, 'Could that have been the reason why he didn't want to do those experiments in the first place?'

'No.' Crawley got up and paced to the window again. 'He didn't want to do them because he suspected that they wouldn't support our preliminary results, which seemed to show a small nutritional advantage from GM crops. There was every chance that they would, in fact, support the findings outlined in Dr Boklova's paper, and the work that others adduced in the discussion after it.'

'So, if Professor Jones knew that his conclusions weren't strongly supported, why was he so eager to publish them?'

'Because he needed the money! Isn't that nearly always the answer to why people act crookedly? Funds for research are increasingly difficult to come by, and the funding we were getting was generous. We hoped it would be extended for another two years, but our funders had their own agenda. They're in the GM crop business. Of course, they have never openly required pro-GM findings as a quid pro quo for funding – they're more subtle than that – but Hywel was afraid that if we knocked the nutritional advantage argument on the head, we wouldn't get any more money.'

'And what did you feel?'

'I didn't go into scientific research in order not to tell the truth. And if that sounds pious, too bad.'

'Good thing you didn't consider going into politics then,' Ian Matthews said, and Paula frowned at him.

'This is very helpful, Dr Crawley,' she said. 'Can you just tell us exactly what was said in your altercation with Professor Jones, as you recall it?'

Crawley ran a hand over his neat hair and gave a weary, almost histrionic, sigh. 'I'm sure you know how unreliable memory is,' he said, 'and feelings were running high. I don't really think—'

'As you remember it, Dr Crawley. I'm sure you must have gone through it in your head afterwards, didn't you?'

He took a half-step forward, as if he was considering returning to his chair, but changed his mind and remained standing, distancing himself as far as he could.

'Hywel challenged Dr Boklova's conclusions at the end of her paper, and, as I remember, it was Dr Varma and Professor Susan Kessler who jumped to Dr Boklova's defence. It got quite rowdy, with Peter Pratt trying to calm things down, and then Dr Varma stirred things further by mentioning our paper and the recommendations of the referees for further work. Hywel completely lost his temper at that point – with some justification. Referees' reports are supposed to be confidential. And then Dr Varma challenged him directly – asked him if those experiments had been done.'

'Which they hadn't,' Ian Matthews said.

Crawley said nothing. He was looking at his feet.

'So what did he say, Dr Crawley?'

He looked up now, the blood rushing into his pale face. 'He pointed at me and asked me if I had done those experiments. It was the most – outrageous thing imaginable. He knew I had not done that work because he had more or less forbidden me to do it.'

132

'So what did you say?'

'Just that. That it had been his decision that those experiments should not be done. And then I walked out. I didn't *storm* out. I left because I had no intention of getting into a slanging match. I think in the circumstances I behaved pretty well.'

'Did you know then about his Alzheimer's diagnosis?'

'No. He hadn't seen fit to inform us. I knew there was something wrong, of course. He had become more erratic, more forgetful, more high-handed.'

'Did it occur to you that he might actually have forgotten that he had decided against doing those experiments?'

'Not at the time. I do wonder now.'

'If so, it must have been humiliating for him to have such an important memory lapse revealed, in public, among his peers.'

Crawley came back to his seat. 'Look,' he said. 'I'm in the dark here. I don't know how he died. *An unexplained death* is all we're told. If he killed himself, don't think for a moment that I'm going to take the blame for humiliating him. I defended myself as I needed to. My career is in the balance here. I stated the facts and then I left . What he did then was up to him.'

'What did you do then?' Ian Matthews asked.

'I went over the road to the pub, drank a whisky, and then went home.' He looked at Ian Matthews. 'Just one whisky, Detective Constable. I was not over the limit.'

'So you spent that night at home, did you?' Ian Matthews asked.

'I did. I didn't hear about Hywel's death until Peter Pratt sent an email round the department the next day.'

'Can anyone vouch for you being at home?'

'I live alone.'

Paula stood up. 'Thank you for your time, Dr Crawley.

That's all we need from you for the moment. We may need to talk again. I take it you'll be here?'

'I shall be clearing my desk and looking for another post.'

'Good luck,' she said.

He held the door open for her, and as she went through, he said, 'With your chemistry degree, did you never think of a career in science?'

'I don't think I could have coped with the drama,' she said.

In the car, leaving the campus, Paula was silent, thinking and willing Ian Matthews not to talk. He seemed to get her unspoken message, and eventually she rewarded him by saying, 'So what did you think of him?'

'I wouldn't trust him. Entitlement written all over him.'

'He's in a fix. It's a dodgy time for him, before he gets a lectureship, a secure long-term job. This half-baked paper that everyone knows about, and now Hywel Jones's suspicious death – hanging around him like a bad smell. I'm not surprised he's feeling hard-done-by.'

'He's the kind of bloke who's had it cushy all his life. Good for him to have to face the real world.'

'All the same,' Paula said.

'I wouldn't put it past him to have done it – killed Jones. He'll have known about his diabetes. He says he went off home but there's no proof of that. He could have hung around.'

'Motive?'

'Fury, resentment, revenge. Hywel Jones had screwed up his career, embarrassed him among the people he needed to impress.'

'I agree he was obviously angry, but angry enough to kill? And what would be the point of killing him while he was asleep? The point about revenge is that the victim has to know about it. That's the satisfaction.'

'Well, we can't be sure that Jones didn't know, can we? We've assumed that he was injected while he was asleep, because that was how he was found, but what was to stop a strong young man from getting hold of him and telling him exactly what he was going to do with him?'

'Crawley doesn't look that strong,' Paula objected. 'He's a bit wimpy, isn't he?'

'Stronger than a sick man thirty years older than him. It would explain those bruises on Jones's arm – where his killer got hold of him. Then he straightens things up to make it all look peaceful – a sad accident.'

'It's a possibility,' Paula said, but a thought was niggling at her that she wasn't going to share with Ian Matthews, because he would take it and run with it like an over-eager prop forward. If Bridget could tear herself away from domestic life, she needed to talk to her.

All she said was, 'We may need to go back to the campus. Crawley wasn't the only person working in that research group. I think I'd like to talk to the others.'

Back at the station she checked the time. Was there any chance that Bridget was free to talk? She decided on coffee in the canteen instead of from the machine, and then she would try phoning her.

Over her coffee she checked her texts, not quite acknowledging that she was hoping for one from Rula. Nothing. She swallowed the last of her coffee, checked the time again and went back to her office.

Bridget answered the call on the second ring. Paula could hear the unmistakeable sounds of an A&E waiting room.

'Am I glad to hear from you,' Bridget said. 'Hold on, I'll slip outside.'

Paula heard her mutter something, presumably to Martin, and then the background noise changed, and she guessed that Bridget was now in a car park.

'Apparently Monday morning is the busiest time in A&E,' Bridget was saying. 'Worse than Saturday night. People don't want to waste their weekend sitting in a hospital, so they wait till Monday and then take the morning off work.'

'Has he been triaged?'

'About an hour ago. Martin's obviously not dying, so it's going to be a long wait. I could do with him to be groaning like he did in the night, but he's gone all stiff upper lip now. I might be able to come in this afternoon if you need me.'

'No, no. You do your wifely duty bit. Take the time you need.'

'To tell you the truth, we can't afford that. Martin won't be back at work any time soon. A builder with a broken foot is no use to anyone. So if we're going to pay the mortgage this month I'll need to do overtime, never mind taking leave.'

'Understood. So there's something I want to run by you.'

'OK. If it's something to think about while we're sitting around, that'd be a bonus.'

'I'm just back from interviewing Dr Alaric Crawley, the guy who had an altercation with Hywel Jones at the conference and walked out.'

'Oh yes? Enlightening or not?'

'I'm not sure. That's why I want your take.'

'I take it you took DC Matthews with you?'

'I did. The two of them took an instant dislike to each other. A bit of a locking of antlers – though Crawley doesn't have much in the way of antlers – he's a bit *effete*, I think is the word.'

'So you want my unprejudiced view?'

'Yes. So this is the story as Crawley tells it.'

It was, Paula realised as she got started, quite a lengthy story, involving explanations of scientific research practice, the publication of papers and the vagaries of funding, before she ever reached the nitty gritty of who claimed to have said what, but Bridget was quick, and they were soon at the crunch point.

'So, the point is this, Bridget. Alaric Crawley had a very public row with Hywel Jones that afternoon, and then disappeared. He says he had a drink in the pub across the road and then packed up and went home. We can check on the drink, but no-one can vouch for him spending the night at home. DC Matthews sees him as slipping back into the college, going to Hywel Jones's room, and pumping insulin into him in fury at his having wrecked his prospects of a stellar career. I don't think he's a man who would take that sort of risk for no advantage except to settle a grudge. Whoever killed Jones wanted to make it look like either an accident or suicide. Crawley was very agitated by the idea that his putting the blame for the missing experiments onto Jones had driven him to kill himself, but that was obviously going to happen in the case of an overdose.'

'So you're ruling Crawley out?' Bridget sounded slightly breathless, and Paula guessed that she was pacing the perimeter of the car park.

'I'm not ruling him out, but I'm thinking of a stronger motive – one that made killing Jones seem imperative, and worth taking risks.'

'I'm with you. Carry on.'

'Crawley told us that Hywel Jones had vetoed doing those further experiments because he suspected that the results would be negative for GM foods, and he was afraid that the GM companies funding them wouldn't feel inclined to extend their funding. But we only have his word for that. When Hywel Jones was asked at the meeting if the additional work recommended by the referees had been done, he asked Crawley if he had done the work. Crawley presented that to us as outrageous – a shameless attempt by Jones to shift the blame for shoddy work away from himself and onto him, but suppose it was the other way round? Crawley had much more to lose if they lost their funding and the research was wound up. Hywel Jones knew he was at the end of his career. He had only just had confirmation of his diagnosis, but he knew he was losing his grip. Funding for another two years' research wasn't crucial for him. But it was for Crawley. This was a critical time for him. In a year's time he'd be applying for full-time university jobs. The success of the work he had done as a postdoc would be crucial. If the project had to be wound up for lack of funding, he'd be at a disadvantage. So, maybe he was the one who saw that those experiments were not going to prove the nutritional advantage of GM crops – quite the reverse, in fact – and he exploited Hywel Jones's increasingly confused state to persuade him to write up the work they had done, and to shelve further experiments when asked to do them, in the hope that Jones would forget about them. And maybe Jones had forgotten, but when he was questioned about them he remembered – and remembered that Crawley was supposed to have done them.'

'That would really put Crawley in the shit.'

'It would. Because now Jones had been reminded, he was unlikely to let it go. Crawley had embarrassed him in front of his peers by claiming that he was responsible for shoddy work. He was unlikely to forget or forgive that. He might well demand a public apology.'

'You're telling a good story, boss. How do you see it going after that?'

'Maybe Crawley does go home – gives himself time to think – or maybe he doesn't. Either way, he knows he has to talk to Hywel Jones. He has to limit the damage. So he goes to see Jones in his room later that evening, hoping to persuade him or bamboozle him into believing that he really had countermanded the further work, and suggesting that they quietly forget about it.'

'But Jones won't play?'

'No. He is a man in a crisis in his life. His mental confusion comes and goes as yet, and he cares about his legacy. This may be his last conference. He's not prepared to leave it with disgrace hanging over him. He wants a public apology.'

'Which would put an end to Crawley's career.'

'It would. So now Crawley has a reason to risk everything by getting rid of Jones, and the opportunity is right there. He knows Jones is diabetic, and he has no trouble giving an injection. He'll have done that sort of thing in the lab.'

'What about prints? Does he wipe down everything in the room? He would need to be very systematic.'

'That's why I think he probably did go home after his drink in the pub. He thought about the situation and picked up a pair of laboratory gloves just in case he had to go for the nuclear option.'

'Would he have the gloves at home?'

'He could have gone into the lab – Saturday night, no-one around.'

Bridget was quiet. Paula could hear her breathing and pacing. 'It's pretty speculative, isn't it?' she said eventually. 'Where would we go for evidence?'

'I want to talk to the others in the research group – see what we can glean about the work, about relations between group members, about what they think of Crawley. And then, if I can make a case, we take in Crawley's lab computer. He has to have written up all his work and results – a complete record. When I was a student we wrote up our research in lab notebooks, which can't be fudged or altered later. Crawley could have tampered with his records but we can run a document history to check that.'

'OK.'

'You don't sound convinced.'

'It's just—'

'Look, Bridget,' Paula said, knowing she was overreacting because she was by no means sure herself, 'it's the best we've got. None of these people look like killers, but this guy's really intense. He looks like someone who could be driven to extremes. And he's a more solid candidate than Dr Boklova's phantom stalker.'

'I need to go back inside,' Bridget said. 'But just one thing. You say that none of them look like killers. So why are we set on it being murder? What about rethinking accident? Or suicide? There's a good motive for that, and a painless means at hand. We could hand it over to the coroner and they'd probably give an open verdict.'

It wasn't fair to be angry. Bridget was tired and worried, and she hadn't met Crawley and heard his story. All the same, Paula felt like snapping.

'Three things. One, the bruising on Hywel Jones's arm. If the autopsy shows those to be fingerprints, then he didn't hold his own arm while he was injecting, did he? Two, you haven't met Ruth Curtis, Hywel Jones's wife. She's an intelligent, sensible woman, and she is certain that he wouldn't have killed himself – that it was against his deeply-held beliefs. And third – well, never mind. It's those two things, really. '

What she didn't say was that her third reason was that Gina Gray believed he had been killed – Gina Gray, whose only knowledge of the case was via her sixteen-year-old granddaughter. Gina Gray, who had no place in this investigation at all.

Chapter Twenty-Four

NEGATIVE FEEDBACK

Monday

'So let me get this straight, DC Cotton.' DCI Ireland's voice was dangerously quiet, and the whole incident room was hushed. 'Cutting to the chase – in a very real sense – you are telling us that you saw the girl, and you lost her?'

All eyes were on Wayne Cotton, who seemed to have shrunk without his usual joker's bravado, and Rula could see that he was beginning to sweat.

'I dunno where she went,' he said. 'I was doing a tour of the nail bars, and I went into this one, and I saw her right away. It was a little slice of a place, narrow but deep, and she was at the far end, mopping the floor. The minute she saw me she dropped the mop and scooted out the back. I scooted after her but she was gone – vanished. There was just a toilet and a bit of a kitchen out there – nowhere to hide – and a door into a yard. I went out there, but there was no way out. There's buildings all round, nowhere you could even climb out.'

'What about upstairs?' Rula asked.

'There was no stairs at the back. The staircase was in the salon. Just to the right as you come in through the door. No way she could have got up there.'

'The cellar,' Tom Ireland said wearily. 'There'll be a cellar. It's probably where she's been sleeping. You didn't think to look for a trapdoor, I suppose?'

Wayne Cotton raised his hands in mute apology and surrender.

'We should get along there, right away,' Meera Javid said, on her feet and ready to go.

Tom Ireland shook his head. 'She'll be long gone,' he said. He looked at Wayne Cotton and asked, 'I assume you questioned the other girls?'

'I did, of course,' Cotton said, 'but they clammed up – *no spick Eengleesh*. We need to get them in here. We'll get them talking then – with an interpreter if need be.'

'That won't work,' Rula said. 'They're probably all trafficked, and they're more scared of their traffickers than they'll ever be of us.'

'I'm putting out the CCTV image of the girl to the media,' Tom Ireland said. 'It's time.'

'Didn't we agree not to because it would put her in danger?' Rula objected.

'She's in danger anyway,' Tom Ireland said. 'And we'll do a search of the nail bar and find that cellar. If she's been moved in a hurry, we may find something.'

'Can I make a suggestion?' Rula asked.

'Nobody has to ask permission to make suggestion here, least of all you,' Tom Ireland said.

'It's a bit way out,' Rula said, 'but if we think we can't get the other girls talking to us, we could get someone in under-cover. Everyone chats while they're having their nails done, don't they?' She looked at her unadorned hands. 'I've never had my nails done, but maybe I should.'

Meera Javid raised a hand, her face glowing with excitement. 'I could do it,' she said. 'They might not be so much on their guard with someone like me. I could tell them a story about an arranged marriage – I've never had my nails done before but I'm meeting my fiancé for the first time and need to make a good impression.'

Rula exchanged looks with Tom Ireland, and he gave the slightest of nods.

'If you do it, Meera,' she said, 'ditch the biker jacket. It doesn't fit the scenario.'

Meera beamed. 'I'll borrow an outfit.' She surveyed her short, slightly ragged nails. 'My mum will be delighted,' she said.

An hour and a half later, as Rula was exercising self-denial and getting a fairly disgusting coffee from a machine, eschewing the better coffee that came with time-wasting chat in the canteen, Meera came powering down the corridor. For a moment, she was unrecognisable in her disguise of salwar kameez and a loose headscarf, but her young voice rang out ahead of her.

'Reporting back!' she called. 'Can we talk?'

Rula knew that she should get her to break the habit of reporting to her, and tell her to find DCI Ireland or wait for the afternoon team debriefing, but she couldn't resist Meera's impatient excitement – and anyway, she wanted to know.

'Do you want a coffee?' she asked.

Meera grimaced. 'That machine is in breach of the Trade Descriptions Act. It has never seen a coffee bean. Hold on–' She rifled in her shoulder bag and produced a tea bag. 'It does hot water. It should manage to make me a mint tea,' she said.

The incident room was quiet, and they settled at Rula's desk.

'You didn't ride your bike in that outfit, did you?' Rula asked.

'I did! These are trousers, after all. Rubber bands round the ankles, though.'

'You must have been quite a sight.'

'I'm not sure anyone noticed. Londoners have seen everything, haven't they?'

'So, the nail bar. What happened?'

Meera blew on her tea, and then took a cautious sip. 'Nothing happened at first,' she said. 'I knew better than to start in with questions, so I had this whole story about my arranged marriage and how I wanted my nails to look nice but not too flashy, because I didn't know what my prospective husband liked. I hoped I could go on to talk about wishing I was free to choose, and I might get some reaction, but either they really didn't understand much English, or they have been drilled in what to talk about and not talk about. There was the girl who was doing my nails and another one – a sort of trainee, I think – who handed her the things she needed. Like a dentist's nurse! All the time I was talking, they were nodding and smiling, but they didn't say anything. And as soon as I stopped, one of them would start a completely different topic. I think they had been given a list to learn of safe openings. So I got, *It's quite a nice day today, isn't it?* and *Are you going on holiday soon?* and – a bit left field – *Do you have any pets?* But I'm not sure if they even understood what they were saying, because when I answered they just did the smiling and nodding thing again, and didn't say anything, even when I did *How about you?'*

'So not much use, except to confirm that they don't get out much. No sign of our girl, I assume?'

'No. And I was getting pretty fed up with talking to myself, but I had to wait for the nails to dry, and then a man came in. He didn't say anything to them, but I could see them stiffen, like they were afraid of him. He went straight upstairs. He looked like he was in a hurry and I guessed he'd be down again in a minute. He wasn't going to say anything to them while I was there, so I paid and left. The girls squawked and flapped a bit – I suppose about the sticky nails – but I got out and waited so I could get a photo of the guy. There was a silver Merc parked on a double yellow just outside, which had to be his. I only had to wait a few minutes, but I was quite glad of the disguise. In that area, if I had been in normal clothes I would have been taken for a tart, hanging around there.'

'And he came out? Did you get a picture?'

'I did. He was carrying a couple of plastic bags of stuff. He put them in the boot, and then walked round to the driver's side, and just as he was about to get in, he stopped and looked around. I took one shot and then ran round the corner and jumped on my bike. I don't know whether he saw me take it, but he couldn't follow me. He was facing the wrong way and the traffic was heavy.'

'Did he look like he could be our guy? I know we don't have much from the chap at the ticket barrier – your friend Mr Small – only *youngish, white, designer stubble.*'

'No.' Meera had her phone out and was scrolling. 'This man was older.'

She passed the phone to Rula, who stared at it. The man was in his fifties, almost bald, with a lined, tight face and wary eyes.

She handed the phone back to Meera.

'I know who he is,' she said.

Chapter Twenty-Five

MISSENSE MUTATION

Tuesday

The logic of adults! Would someone explain it to her, please?

Yes, she had lost it in Mrs Mancini's office yesterday, ambushed by a flood of embarrassing tears that she wasn't prepared for, and it had been excruciatingly awkward. But all she wanted to do then was to splash some cold water on her face, sit in the common room for a bit, and then go back to lessons. Instead, Mrs Mancini had more or less imprisoned her in her office, and then – without her permission, which she was sure wasn't even legal – she had rung her mum, at work, to tell her that she thought Freda should go home, and perhaps see her GP. So then there was Mum arriving, all flustered and guilty, rushing her off home, phoning the doctor. Of course there were no appointments for people whose only symptoms were that they had been crying – didn't they know the NHS was in crisis mode? – so the upshot was that the adults who were supposed to be looking after her welfare had decided that instead of going to school, where there were other things to think about and friends to talk to, she was stuck at home, on her own because neither Mum nor Ben could take time off work to sit here watching her in case she started crying again. What she needed was *a bit of a rest and some peace and quiet* they said. Well, bollocks to that.

She picked up her phone, dialled, and was answered on the first ring.

'Freda? What's the matter? Are you all right?'

Oh, not her too. Would people please just stop worrying about her!

'Of course I'm all right, Granny. Why wouldn't I be?'

'Well, I may be a bit out of it at the moment, but even I can see that it is nine-thirty on a Tuesday morning in term-time, and you are phoning me rather than discussing *The Mill on the Floss* or being creative in the art room. Also, you stumbled on a dead person two days ago, so I think I'm entitled to ask if you're all right.'

She was sounding better, Freda thought, more like her usual self.

'It's *Middlemarch* we're doing, actually,' she said.

'Well, that's a tougher challenge than *The Mill*, but it's hardly a reason for bunking off school.'

'I am not bunking off! It's not my choice. I'm being made to stay at home, so my poor, frail nerves can recover.'

'That doesn't sound like a bad idea.'

'It is. I'm bored.'

'So you thought you'd kill the time by phoning me.'

'No! I didn't mean it to sound like that. I wanted to know if there was any news about David, of course.'

'There is no news. He spent another *comfortable night*, for which there is no evidence, since he isn't communicating, but I've stopped arguing. And I am still in Stourly because this nasty little pub suits my mood.'

'Aren't you bored?'

'I defy boredom. As I used to tell your mother and Auntie Annie when they whined about being bored, *If you're bored it's because you're boring.*'

'You must have been quite annoying.'

'Oh, I was. I was.'

'Anyway, you wouldn't like a trip into Marlbury, would you? We could meet up and—'

'I would love to see you, darling, but I dare not go into Marlbury. Don't forget, my name has been in all the papers, and there are too many people who might recognise me. You could come here, though. I'll pay your train fare, and if you can get here before eleven, I'll take you for brunch at my favourite café.'

The day was looking up. 'You're on,' Freda said.

Chapter Twenty-Six

FEEDBACK INHIBITION

Tuesday

There is something Freda isn't telling me. I can believe that Ellie fussed and the school was anxious to be seen to be doing the right thing, but it's not easy to bully Freda, and I don't believe she would have put up with being made to stay at home without a fight – not just at the beginning of her A level courses, when everything is new and daunting. So what is going on? I will find out. I shall feed her and lull her, and she will tell me all.

I look and smell disgusting. I haven't showered or changed my clothes since I met Ruth Curtis on Sunday. I have slept in most of my clothes because I have told myself that I shall need to set off instantly if I am summoned by the hospital. It makes no sense, of course, because there are no trains in the middle of the night. It is just an excuse. I just can't be bothered.

So, I must make an effort. My bathroom is as unwelcoming as the rest of this establishment – cold, grubby and short of places to put or hang anything – but I brave it, and stand under the trickle of barely warm water that the shower grudgingly emits, washing my hair vigorously. I get into clean underwear, get back into my much lived-in trousers, as I have no alternative, but improve things by adding a new top, bought on my foray into M&S three endless days ago. I towel-dry my hair as I can't find a hairdryer anywhere in the room, and I sit down to put some makeup on, though this is not going to fool Freda. My face is horrible – pale and blotchy, with a crop of spots on my chin and new wrinkles round my eyes, which have sprung from nowhere. I am a wreck.

Fortunately, there is enough sun to justify sunglasses, so when Freda texts to tell me what time her train gets in, I text back that I will meet her at the station. I won't be able to keep the glasses on in the café, but it is quite dark in there – part of its olde worlde charm – and I can hope to find us a shadowy corner.

Freda looks fine when she jumps off the train, wearing jeans and T-shirt, and with her hair freshly straightened (the straighteners a birthday present from me). We hug, and set off for the café. I must not rush to find out what is going on with her, so I turn our thoughts to brunch and the choices to be made. I realise that for the first time in three days I actually feel hungry. It's not that I'm feeling any better, I think, but just my body asserting itself and demanding sustenance.

'I think I'll have croque monsieur,' I say, and Freda, who is in a vegetarian phase, wonders if they will do her a croque monsieur without ham, but with mushrooms on the side.

'I'm sure they will,' I say, 'or you could have a croque madame without ham.'

'What does that have?'

'A poached egg on the top.'

'Yuk!' she says.

'Do you remember all those eggs we had to keep eating when we were staying with Eve during lockdown?' I say.

'I do. And you over-ordered on avocados, remember.'

'I did. It was a funny time, wasn't it? It feels like a dream now.'

'It was unique,' she says. 'And crazy. All that singing we did while we walked the dogs!'

'I knitted a blanket.'

'And we rescued that woman. When we went back to school most people complained that it had been boring, but we were never bored, were we?' She pauses. 'Mum was so cross that I'd had a good time. In her world, her children can only be happy if they are with her.'

This might be a moment to ask her why she has given in to Ellie's making her stay at home, but I can't speak. I am experiencing something like a wave of panic. I am assaulted by a vivid memory of arriving home after our months in lockdown, and finding David there, with my accumulated mail neatly sorted into piles, and tea and doughnuts at the ready. It knocks the breath out of me and it is all I can do not to crumple at the knees and sit on the pavement and howl. I don't do that. Instead I take hold of Freda's arm. I try to make it seem just an affectionate sort of semi-hug, but she is onto it. She is half a head taller than me these days, and she puts her arm round my shoulders and holds me up as she steers me into the café.

When we are settled in a corner, and the nice French waitress comes to take our order, Freda takes over, ordering the croque monsieurs, negotiating the side order of mushrooms, and, without consultation, asking for two large cappuccinos. I would have gone for an espresso, but she is probably right that the cappuccinos will be more comforting.

By the time this is done, my breathing is nearly normal and we smile at each other, complicit in the understanding that something just happened that we are not going to talk about.

'So,' I say, '*Middlemarch*. That's a big ask for your first A level text. I think I'd have left it to the second year.'

'Mr Murray says it's one of the greatest English novels.'

'So it is. But it is hard. How far have you got?'

'We had to read it over the summer.'

'Did everyone do it?'

'If they didn't they're doing a good job of blagging it.'

'So what do you think of it?'

'I don't know yet. I got so frustrated with Dorothea, thinking Casaubon was this great man, when he's obviously a complete fake. And then there's Rosamonde Viney, whose husband really is rather great, and she moans about him because he doesn't earn enough money. And I could have said that yesterday when Mr Murray asked me, but instead I just gaped at him like an idiot.'

'Not like you. Why did you gape?'

'Because my mind was somewhere else, and that can happen to anyone, but suddenly it's a big issue, and Mr Murray is talking to Mrs Mancini, who does pastoral care, and she's talking to Mum, and it's a whole thing, and here I am on some kind of sick leave.'

At this point, our food and drinks arrive, and this gives me some thinking time. I am still wondering why Freda hasn't talked about kicking up a fuss about the sick leave. We both dig into our nicely oozing toasted brioche, and when we have made appropriate murmurs of pleasure, I say, 'Presumably you told Mrs Mancini about what happened in the English lesson – that you just had a mind wandering moment?'

'Of course,' she says, without taking her eyes off her food. 'These mushrooms are delish.'

I am not to be diverted. 'So how did she manage to turn a moment's inattention into a cause for phoning your mum at work and signing you off school? It sounds barmy.'

She says something I can't hear, her head down and her mouth full of food.

'What?' I ask.

She looks up. 'I blubbed,' she says. 'For no reason. I just blubbed. And then I was so humiliated I couldn't argue back, and every time I tried to say I was all right, I started crying again. It was the most embarrassing thing in my whole life.'

'Delayed shock,' I say.

'That's what they said. Mum wants to take me to the doctor, but I absolutely refuse. Because it's not shock, and I can't tell them what it is because Mum will get all anxious and think I'm trying to find out what happened to Faith's dad.'

'You can tell me,' I say. 'I have too much else to be anxious about to worry about you doing some sleuthing.'

'I saw something,' she says. 'I know I saw something that morning when we found him. It was something important but I can't remember what it was, and it's driving me mad. That's what I was thinking about in English instead of Rosamond Viney, and it's what stops me sleeping, and I don't know what to do to remember it.'

'Well, being stuck at home isn't going to help. You need to be distracted, and then when you're thinking about something else it will come to you. Do you want me to have a word with your mum?'

'No. She'll get annoyed. I'm going back to school tomorrow whether they like it or not. We've got a meeting about designing the set for the Christmas play.'

'What's the play?'

'*Little Women*.'

'Good choice.'

We pick up our knives and forks and finish eating in silence. I don't know what Freda's thoughts are, but I am thinking that she isn't the only one with a niggling half memory. Ever since we sat down here, I have wrestled with a powerful conviction that something important is now clear to me, if only I knew what it was.

Chapter Twenty-Seven

NEGATIVE FEEDBACK

Tuesday

'I don't believe it! I don't bloody believe it!'

Paula glared at the sheet of paper that Bridget was holding out to her.

'Came in overnight,' Bridget said. 'I just printed it off.'

Reluctantly, Paula took the autopsy report and scanned it. There it was: *Insulin was injected into the upper left arm. Bruises below the injection site are consistent with the arm's having been grasped tightly before or during the injection process. Clear finger marks are visible. The marks are small, and more likely to be a woman's than a man's.*

'Lets our posh friend Dr Crawley off the hook,' Bridget said.

'And we've let the women out of the country,' Paula wailed. 'Irina Boklova, Ceren Alkan, the diabetic American woman – Susan something – and her bodyguards. Even the Indian woman who rowed with Hywel Jones at the meeting. We hardly bothered with her, did we? And we can't get them back, not without solid evidence against them.'

'It rules out Yilmaz,' Bridget said. 'He's a chunky sort of chap. Fat fingers I bet.'

Paula looked at her with dawning hope. '*More likely to be a woman's than a man's,*' she said. 'The report doesn't say those bruise's couldn't have been from a man, and Alaric Crawley has this habit of running his hand over his very neat hair. I noticed what a feminine gesture it looked on him, because he had little hands.'

'Like Donald Trump,' Bridget said.

'Don't!' Paula said.

She paced around the small area of the office that allowed for pacing. 'Right,' she said. 'A two-pronged approach. I'm not giving up on Crawley, and I haven't forgotten that Gina Gray thinks Irina Boklova or Direnç Yilmaz is involved. I'm going to talk to the others in Hywel Jones's research group, and it'll be a good idea for you to talk to Gina. She might be less guarded with you. There's something she was going to tell me before she changed her mind. And talk to her granddaughter too – Freda. Get her to go over her story about Jones groping Ceren Alkan, because at the moment Irina Boklova has no motive, apart from a professional disagreement – and those don't usually lead to murder.'

'A pat on the bottom isn't much of a motive either,' Bridget objected.

'No. But she is very protective of Dr Alkan. Which reminds me, have we tracked down that Turkish mobile that made calls to Irina Boklova's phone? If we're ruling Yilmaz out then we need to know who else was trying to contact her.'

'We're on it,' Bridget said, 'but the Turkish police aren't very co-operative.'

'You amaze me,' Paula said.

Chapter Twenty-Eight

LOSS POTENTIAL

Tuesday

'So, people, we have a name! The first piece of solid fact that we've had. We're all sorry that DC Cotton managed to scare off our key witness, but DS Javid has managed to save us from looking like a bunch of amateurs. We now have a photo of a man who came into the nail bar where our witness was seen. He was clearly at home there. He went up to the floor above and removed a carrier bag of material before leaving. DS Javid took a photo of him, and DI Bartosz recognised it.'

With a flourish, Tom Ireland fixed a printout to the evidence board. 'Does anyone else know who this is?' he asked.

He was met with blank looks.

'You've none of you been here long enough. You're too young,' Tom Ireland said. 'Who is he, DI Bartosz?'

Feeling old, Rula said, 'Former DS Brian Drake. Resigned from the force five years ago.'

'And why did he resign?'

'Officially, on medical advice. Burn out.'

'And unofficially?'

'There was a disciplinary. A dossier of evidence was presented, which included taking bribes, falsifying evidence, and rape and sexual assault.'

'And do we know who was responsible for driving the inquiry that produced that dossier?'

'It was DCI David Scott – as he was then.'

A little ripple of reaction from the room.

'And what was the conclusion of the disciplinary hearing?' Tom Ireland asked.

'It went up to the highest level,' Rula said, working hard at keeping her tone neutral. 'The top brass decided that it was not in the Met's best interests to move to a criminal prosecution. It would be bad for the image, and undermine public trust. He was allowed to resign citing medical problems, but he didn't get early retirement. He'll have to wait for his pension.'

'Poor chap,' Tom Ireland said. 'So how's he to make a living? Employers tend to be wary of an ex-cop who doesn't have a convincing story about why he's ex. But, fortunately for him, he's made some friends in the criminal community during his time helping to keep London safe, and he has no trouble finding himself a niche there. I think we shall find that nail bar isn't his only business interest. There'll be others – and they're just the front windows, of course. Brothels, illegal betting, drug distribution – and slavery, because the whole thing will depend on a constant stream of trafficking victims, like our missing girl.'

As he stopped, a buzz of conversation started, but Tom Ireland raised a hand. 'We can't get too excited yet,' he called above the chatter. 'Two things. One is he's not going to be easy to find. Thanks to DC Cotton, he'll be rattled. He'll know we've searched those premises. They'd been cleared out by the time we got there, including upstairs, which he must have used as some kind of office. There was a safe, and

I guess its contents went out with him in the carrier bag. The other thing is he's changed his name. Turns out the address we turned up is his ex-wife's place, and she says she hasn't seen him – or any support for the kids – since she divorced him five years ago. I'm inclined to believe her because when DI Bartosz went to the house, she was admitted by a good-looking man who clearly lived there. The wife has definitely moved on. We shall find him, though. That at least, we're good at, and that's first business for anyone who wants to do some overtime this evening.'

As the meeting started to break up, Rula raised an arm and called above the hubbub.

'One more thing, guys. If Mr Small, the ticket collector, is to be believed, Brian Drake isn't our prime suspect. The man he saw with the girl coming off the Dover train was younger. Brian Drake is in his fifties and looking older, to judge from his photo. We need to find him, but that's not going to be the end of it.'

Chapter Twenty-Nine

FLUID MOSAIC MODEL

Tuesday

Freda's mobile rang as she was on the train back to Marlbury. She fished it out of her pocket, guessing it was her mother checking up on her, but found that it was from a mobile number she didn't know. She decided not to answer, but it rang again immediately. Perhaps this was some sort of emergency.

'Hello,' she said.

'Is that Freda Gray?' a woman's voice asked.

'Who are you?' Freda said. It sounded rude, she knew, but she had found that it was quite effective with scammers. It took them off their script.

'I'm DS Bridget O'Malley from Marlbury police,' the voice said, and Freda felt it was a reassuring voice, while at the same time thinking that if this was a journalist trying to find Granny, she would be reassuring, wouldn't she?

'How do I know that's true?' she said.

'Quite right to be cautious,' the woman said. 'I was hoping we could have a talk, and then I can show you my ID. I'm on the team investigating the death of Professor Hywel Jones. I know you have already answered some questions from my boss, DI Paula Powell, but I would like to have another chat, if that's all right with you.'

'Why?' Freda asked. 'When I've already told DI Powell everything.'

'Sometimes we remember things later that we didn't remember in the shock of the event.'

If only you knew, Freda thought. *And if only I thought talking to you would help.*

'All right,' she said.

'Where are you, actually?' Bridget O'Malley asked. 'I rang now because I thought you might be on your lunch break at school, but you sound as though you're on a train.'

'I've been given time off school. For shock.'

'I see. So where are you going on a train?'

'I've just been to see my gran,' she said defensively, and then she could have torn her tongue out. *Too much information*. Randomly, she added, 'But she's gone to London now.'

'I see,' Bridget O'Malley said, although Freda thought she couldn't possibly see. 'Well, look. If you tell me when your train gets in, I could meet you at the station. We could have a chat in the car, or we could go to the cafeteria. Have a coffee.'

'All right,' Freda said, thinking that all important conversations these days seemed to come with a hot drink.

She had no trouble spotting DS O'Malley when she got off the train. She was wearing a belted raincoat that would have looked right on any TV detective. Her hair was unexpected, though – curly, and the sort of classy reddish brown that dyed red hair never managed. She had no trouble identifying Freda either, but that didn't make her a great detective, since Freda was the only teenage girl on the platform.

'Freda!' she said, and shook her hand. 'The café looks a bit crowded for a confidential chat. Do you mind talking in the car?'

'Is it a squad car?' Freda asked. If she was spotted in a police car, the Marlbury gossip lines would be working overtime.

'No. I'm a detective,' DS O'Malley said. 'My car is in plain clothes too.'

When they were in the perfectly ordinary grey car, Freda said, 'I did tell DI Powell everything I could remember. I don't think I've got anything else to add.'

'I know.' DS O'Malley had taken a tablet out of her bag and was scanning it. 'You gave a very helpful account of finding Professor Jones, and it tallies with the accounts that your friends gave, but I'm interested in anything you might have noticed and not registered at the time. In the shock of the moment we notice only the important things, but afterwards we may begin to remember other things, so I'm just going to take you through it and ask a few questions. Is that all right?'

Freda liked this woman's accent. There was something warm and friendly about it. If it had been her who interviewed her on Sunday morning, instead of pissy DI Powell, it would have been a whole different thing.

'OK,' she said.

'Right. So, you were sharing a room with Faith Curtis? Had you two chosen to share?'

'No. There was a double and a single room for the three of us, so we drew lots.'

'Right. So Lisa Baron woke you both up?'

'No. We were awake already. The light from Faith's laptop woke me up.'

'What was she doing on her laptop at that hour of the morning?'

'Tweaking her UCAS form. The upper sixth are all obsessed with their forms at the moment.'

'So Lisa found you both awake, and what did she say?'

'She spoke to Faith really – because it was her stepdad. I don't exactly remember, but she said something like, *You've got to come. Just come.*'

'So she didn't ask you to come? It was Faith she wanted?'

'Well, yes.'

'But you went anyway. Why was that?'

'Well, it was obvious something pretty bad had happened. I suppose I thought I ought to help.'

'And it was a drama, wasn't it? Someone recently said to me, *A drama is catnip to teenage girls.* Do you think that's true?'

'It probably is for girls who haven't had much drama in their lives,' Freda said. 'Not so much if they've had their own dramas, I should think.'

'But you've had your own dramas, haven't you? I've got a note here about your granddad last year. That must have been upsetting.'

'Yes. Of course,' Freda said.

DS O'Malley was scrolling. 'And in 2019 you were kidnapped. There was a nationwide alert and you were found unharmed. Do you want to tell me about that?'

'Not really,' Freda said. 'It's a long story, and it's not relevant, is it?'

'Well, no, except what I'm trying to get at is why you went with the other girls. Lisa had come to get Faith, hadn't she? Why did you feel you could tag along?'

Freda resented *tag along*. She was beginning to feel that she didn't like this woman as much as she had thought she would.

'Lisa was obviously really upset,' she said, 'and she's my friend. I thought I might be able to help.'

'Yes. I can see you like to be helpful, don't you? You're the one who rang 999. But we'll come to that. You followed the other two to Professor Jones's room, and you all went in.'

'No, I didn't go in.'

'You didn't?'

'No. Like you said, Lisa came looking for Faith, not me, so I stayed outside. But then they called me in because they couldn't find his pulse.'

'Which of them called you in? Can you remember?'

Freda thought. 'Actually, I just went in. I could see that they didn't know how to feel for a pulse, and I'd done a first aid course, so I said to try in his neck, and then Faith said something like, *You try*, and I went over to the bed, and I couldn't feel anything.'

'So what did you do then?'

'I said I'd call 999.'

'Wasn't that odd? Wouldn't most girls have found an adult to take over?'

Freda turned away and looked out of the car window. 'DI Powell made a big thing of that,' she said. 'As though it was suspicious somehow. I've been thinking about it, because I can see that it might seem odd. What I think is, we were all working for the first time – doing a paid job – and people were treating us like grown-ups – Alice, the housekeeper, certainly was – so I suppose we felt we had to be adult. There was nobody obvious to go to and I thought it was urgent to get an ambulance. I suppose I thought they might find a pulse, or be able to resuscitate him. We couldn't just decide he was dead because I said so, could we?'

DS O'Malley nodded. 'I can see that,' she said. 'So you called 999. On your mobile? Where did you do that?'

'In our room. My phone was there.'

'Did either of the others come with you?'

'No, they stayed with – in the room.'

'When you'd called, what did you do then? Did you go and join the others?'

'No. I think I expected that Faith would come back – that she'd want to get dressed.'

'Is that what you did?'

'Yes. I went to the bathroom, then got dressed. And then I tidied the room.'

'Really?'

'Yes. I'd forgotten that I did that. I suppose it sounds a bit weird. I think I was wanting to be useful. Or perhaps I was pretending things were normal.'

'What sort of tidying?'

'Nothing much really. I just closed Faith's laptop and made our beds. Then I took our cocoa mugs from the night before and I went down to the kitchen because it was my turn to put things out for the breakfast buffet.'

'That sounds cool, but I'd say you were in shock. Didn't you want to talk to your mum?'

'Not really. She worries. She didn't want me to do the job really, and she'd have panicked.'

'Did you ring her later?'

'Yes. And she panicked – sent my stepdad to fetch me.'

DS O'Malley laughed. 'I'd better get you home,' she said, 'before she finds you gone and panics again.'

As she was driving Freda back home, she said, 'There was one other thing I wanted to ask about. Something you told DI Powell about Dr Alkan throwing water at Professor Jones. Can you tell me what exactly he had done to deserve that?'

'He stroked her bottom.'

'And she threw water at him? Did you think it was a bit extreme?'

'I thought it was cool. Zero tolerance. That's how we girls deal with groping.'

'It's a nice school, yours. Do you still get groping?'

'Oh yes.'

'So how do you deal with it?'

'Stamping on their feet is good. They like to come up behind you and pinch your bum, or get you round the waist, so I stamp back really hard on their foot, and then say, *Oh sorry, I didn't realise anyone was so close.*

DS O'Malley laughed, and then said, 'You told me that Dr Boklova saw the incident and looked annoyed.'

'Yes. I should think they're pretty zero tolerance at Berkely, wouldn't you?'

'Did you know she and Dr Alkan are a couple? So she might have been more than annoyed, mightn't she?'

'I suppose,' Freda said. 'But no-one ever got killed because they stroked someone's bottom, did they?'

Chapter Thirty

PASSIVE IMMUNITY

Tuesday

Will people please stop asking things of me? Can nobody see that it is as much as I can do to put myself to bed and get up again in the morning? Can I not have a life crisis in peace?

Now bloody Paula is onto me again. She sent her sidekick in the hope of catching me off guard, but I know when I'm being targeted. Bridget O'Malley the sidekick is called, and for those who deal in clichés, she is confusing – pre-Raphaelite auburn curls combined with a boring M&S raincoat, and the shamrock name combined with no-nonsense Brummy vowels. She made me think of a character in a Tom Stoppard fantasy novel from the 1960s – *Lord Malquist and Mr Moon*. As I remember it, Lord Malquist has a black coachman with an Irish name, who speaks Yiddish. I may have misremembered the details, but you get the point.

DS O'Malley was perfectly nice – obviously used to playing nice cop to Paula's sarky one – but she wanted to dig away again at the Yilmaz saga, and why I had thought it relevant to remind DI Powell about that aspect of Dr Boklova's history. I burbled on about its always being useful to have the complete story, and then, when she persevered,

I pleaded emotional turmoil and exhaustion, and that shut her up. Because really, what is the point? If Irina did have anything to do with Hywel Jones's death, it's too late to get her, isn't it? That ship has, almost literally, sailed. Irina and Ceren are snugly back in California, and it would take a solid case against them, and a fight with a phalanx of expensive lawyers, to have them hauled back here. And besides, I am less and less convinced that Hywel Jones's death wasn't suicide or accident, and I'll tell you why.

Accident first. Well, it's all very well for Ruth Curtis to talk about muscle memory and the precautions he always took, but the man had dementia. The whole point about dementia is that people are not themselves. They don't do what's usual. They fill the kettle with milk and put coffee in the teapot; they blow up the microwave, and they can't find the front door in the house they've lived in for twenty years. Ruth may think that Hywel hadn't yet got to that stage, but he had had a very demanding, embarrassing, and ultimately humiliating afternoon. He will have been less himself than usual.

And suicide. This has been in my mind more than I want it to be. I don't have the expert medical knowledge to back it up, but I feel sure that the longer someone stays in a coma, the longer they will take to recover. And they may never recover properly. At worst, they stay in some sort of semi-life, and I am obsessed now with the question of who, if it comes to it, makes the decision whether to switch off life support. When I told that triage nurse that I was David's next of kith, it was true. I really don't think he has any next of kin. I have never heard him mention aunts, uncles or cousins, and if they exist, they certainly don't see him or know him. But do I have any say? I am wondering whether police officers have to register their next of kin somewhere, in case of serious injury or death in the line of duty. You would think so, wouldn't you? I suppose initially David would have put his parents' names down, and perhaps he never updated. Or might I find that, at some point, he replaced them with me? Wouldn't he have asked me first, or at least told me? Not necessarily. Given my reaction on the one occasion he asked me to marry him, he might have thought I would shy away from that commitment too. So, I don't know, but I am as sure as I can be that David would want me to pull the plug, and if he had any control over his own body he would choose not to live a helpless, dependent life without any prospect of recovery. But we have never talked about it, so how do I deal with the possibility that I might be wrong?

I know I am making this all about me, when I am supposed to be thinking about Hywel Jones, but what I am saying is that I have only his wife's word for it that he was full of fight and ready to see his decline through to the bitter end. I know she says that his religious belief was against suicide, but beliefs don't always translate into action, do they? Italy is full of Roman Catholics but it has the lowest birth rate in Europe. *Go figure*, as they like to say on *The West Wing*.

I can absolutely believe that Ruth was ready to care for him. She had seen her first husband through his final illness and she was prepared to do it again, but what about him? Couldn't the humiliation of Saturday have made him see the future as it would really be, stripped of the fighting talk? In his work, he had lost track of experiments that should have been done, and had been publicly exposed. And on top of that he had publicly groped a colleague, and had been publicly punished. Freda says he never behaved like that with Faith or her friends, and if he could resist nubile sixteen-year-olds, then I would guess he was not a habitual groper. So wouldn't he have shocked himself when he realised what he had done? And if he was going to put an end to it, that night was the best time to do it, away from home, without his wife to see what he was doing, or to wake in the morning to find him.

I did say some of this to DS O'Malley, because I am not sure that I should have pressed Ruth Curtis's views on Paula. I was impressed by Ruth's vehemence, but now, if I were Paula, I would opt for the easy answer of suicide. But she probably hasn't paid any attention to me, anyway, and she can make her own judgment, can't she?

Chapter Thirty-One

FRAMESHIFT MUTATION

Tuesday

'Zilch. You?'

'Pretty much zilch.'

Paula and Bridget were having their own end of the day debrief, slumped disconsolately in Paula's office.

'Did you get to see the other people in the research group?' Bridget asked.

'Yep. Two men and a woman. Unless they are very good liars, they all like Alaric Crawley. The men agree that he's a bit entitled. But reckon it's justified. He's very clever and very hard-working. They say he's a good colleague and always ready to help. They're PhD students while he's a postdoc, so he's more experienced. They don't know in detail about the missing experiments because they're working from a different angle on the research, but they were aware of the tensions over them . They back up Crawley's line – that Jones was too much in hock to his sponsors and wanted to avoid unwelcome results.'

'What about the woman?'

'She liked him. Said he was a welcome change from most of the men she met – *none of the three Ps.*'

'*Three Ps?*'

'He's not patronising, paranoid or predatory.'

Bridget laughed. 'Not predatory is interesting. Did you ask her if Hywel Jones had ever tried anything with her?'

'No. I was interested in Crawley. Why?'

'Just something Freda Gray said.'

'I thought you said zilch from her.'

'There wasn't anything really. She told the same story she had told you. But when I asked her about the groping and water-throwing incident, we got onto how we deal with groping, and she talked about her friends at school and their *zero tolerance* policy. The girls push back. Freda said she dealt with approaches from behind by stamping back and crushing their toes.'

'And approaches from the front?'

'I didn't ask."

'Well that's all very admirable,' Paula said, 'and I can absolutely believe it of Freda Gray, but how is it relevant?'

'I was just thinking about Hywel Jones and his wandering hands, and those bruises on his arm from female fingers. Suppose they're nothing to do with the insulin – just a woman fending him off very firmly.'

Paula thought. 'It's possible. We could get forensics to look again at the bruises and work out what sort of a hold they suggest.'

'There's another thing,' Bridget said.

'What?'

'You know you said there were three reasons to make this a murder investigation?'

'There were the bruises, and there was Jones's wife's testimony about his attitude to suicide,' Paula said. 'What was my third?'

'That Gina Gray thought it was murder, and her hunches were usually good.'

'Oh, well – that was just—'

'She's changed her mind,' Bridget said. 'She's saying now that she's sorry she brought up the Yilmaz case and wasted our time.'

'That sounds remarkably unlike Mrs Gray. What game is she playing?'

'I don't think she's playing any games,' Bridget said. 'To me she just sounded as though she's at the end of her rope.'

Chapter Thirty-Two

DELETION

Wednesday

Rula stood at a basin in the washroom and inspected her face. She had brushed and retied her hair, and she had splashed cold water on her face, but to anyone who was interested in interpreting, the face shouted *all-nighter*. In the end, tracking down Brian Drake had not been that difficult. He was using an alias, but he hadn't gone the route of a complete new identity, and following the money trail from the purchase of the nail bar premises had yielded an address eventually. At four o'clock that morning they had it, but there was no transport running to go home for some sleep, and anyway, she wanted to be in at the kill. The arrest had been as good as she had hoped – the man bleary-eyed and blustering in his boxers – and now, after they had let him stew for a bit, she was going in with DCI Ireland for the interview. She bared her teeth at herself in the mirror, in the snarling dog grimace that her nieces liked to squeal at, and swung out of the room.

Drake was still blustering when Rula and Tom Ireland walked into the interview room. He stood up and offered a hand.

'Tom! DCI now, I gather. Good stuff.'

Tom Ireland ignored the hand, but Drake carried on. 'And?' He turned to Rula. 'I know your face, of course. Never forget a pretty face, but don't recall the name.'

Rula said nothing, and Tom Ireland turned on the recorder. 08.35 am, interview commencing. DCI Ireland and DI Bartosz interviewing Brian Edward Drake.'

He sat down, with Rula beside him, and looked at Drake across the table that divided them.

'I haven't got time to waste, Mr Drake, so I'll get straight to the point. You have been arrested on charges of people trafficking and false imprisonment. There will be other charges too, I've no doubt, once we have searched your other premises. Your using an alias and forcing us to track you down was inconvenient to us, but it also gave us a pretty good idea of your nasty little business empire.'

Drake opened his mouth to protest, but Tom Ireland held up a hand, and like the magician turning to his female assistant, turned to Rula and gave her a nod. She emptied onto the table the brown A4 envelopes that had been retrieved from Drake's house that morning. Onto the table tumbled passports of various colours, documents in various languages, and a pitiful handful of banknotes in various currencies.

'These were recovered from your home this morning,' Tom Ireland said. They were in plain sight. I'm guessing they Tom what you took from your office above the Sheep Street nail bar when you knew we were onto you. You hadn't found a new hiding place, had you?'

Drake glanced at the pile on the table, and then, just a beat too late, he leant back in his chair and opened his arms in an expansive gesture.

'I'm a philanthropist,' he said. 'I look after the helpless. I give them jobs; I give them somewhere to live. OK, so they may not have been okayed by the Home Office, but are you telling me I'm a criminal for helping them?'

Rula ran her hands over the passports and documents. 'And in return for the jobs and the accommodation, you take their passports, their papers and their money. How does that work exactly?'

He shrugged. 'The accommodation isn't always as good as I'd like. Not much privacy. I keep their stuff safe for them.'

'Very thoughtful,' Rula said, 'but what interests me is that among this stuff I don't see any asylum applications, any letters from lawyers, any evidence that the *help* you are offering includes helping them to settle here legally and securely. Surely you must be doing that if you are such a philanthropist?'

Drake shrugged again. 'Dealing with the Home Office – a nightmare. Go that route and they'll be packed off to so-called hotels. Or Rwanda, of course.' He laughed.

Rula felt temper rising in her, threatening to choke her. 'So they are completely in your power,' she started to say, but she stopped as she felt Tom Ireland stir beside her.

He took a passport from the pile. 'We are going to want answers to DI Bartosz's questions, and a lot more, and I'm sure we shall get them, but at this moment we have a more pressing question. We need to find this girl.' He read from the passport: 'Leila Ebeid, Syrian citizen, aged fifteen. We believe that she was a witness to the attack on Detective Superintendent David Scott four days ago, we need to speak to her urgently, and we are quite sure that you know where she is.'

Brian Drake tried his big, arms-out gesture again, but with less conviction this time, Rula thought.

'Sorry, can't help you,' he said. 'I gather she got spooked by one of your plods coming into the salon. Plain clothes but screamed *cop*. Even a foreigner could spot him. You lot need to do better.'

Rula looked at him. 'It wouldn't take much to make someone leave that little rat hole in the cellar where you were keeping her,' she said.

He shrugged. 'Better than sleeping on the street for a young girl.'

'So you keep her safe, do you? What does she do for you in return, Mr Drake? Because she doesn't paint nails, does she?'

Tom Ireland cleared his throat. 'The thing is, Brian,' he said, and Rula was startled at the sudden change in his tone. 'The thing is, you and I know that you're going down. Trafficking and false imprisonment are just a start. We'll get you on living off immoral earnings as well – and then there'll be drugs, because there are always drugs, aren't there? You will go down, and I don't have to tell you what life is like for a cop inside, but co-operate with us in catching David Scott's attacker, and a good lawyer will find you grounds for leniency. It's the best I can offer you. We don't think you attacked him yourself – you don't match the description we've got – but I think his attacker works for you, and you know who he is. So, tell us what you know, and tell us where our witness is, and make things easier for yourself, why don't you?'

Rula watched, fascinated, as an expression of such pure hatred came over Brian Drake's face that she felt herself shiver.

'Leniency?' he said. 'For trafficking? Don't make me laugh. People traffickers, they're as bad as terrorists, according to the politicians. Prosecute me if you like – if it's easier than going after the real crims – but don't take me for a fool.'

He leant forward, and the PC on guard at the door stepped forward, alert for trouble, but Brian Drake was putting all his aggression into words.

'David Scott is a self-righteous prick,' he hissed. 'He had it in for me for years, and he lost the force a good officer. He was so holier-than-thou that he never understood that I had contacts with crims because that got me results. I hate the bastard. I didn't try to kill him and I don't know who did, but I wouldn't tell you anyway.'

Tom Ireland stood up. 'We tried the carrot, Mr Drake,' he said, 'and you didn't want it, so here's the stick. If it turns out that you know where our witness, Leila Ebaid, is, and you haven't told us, and we find that DSu Scott's attacker works for you, then we'll add conspiracy to murder to your charge sheet, and God himself won't get you leniency then.'

Taken by surprise, Rula jumped to her feet too, but before they turned to walk to the door, Tom Ireland's phone buzzed with an incoming message, and he stopped to look at it. There was something about his intentness as he read it that made Rula hold her breath. Even Brian Drake, she noticed, was watching him. Then he handed the phone to Rula, and spoke to Brian Drake.

'It seems that a young girl's body has been found on the river bank. She had no identification on her, but from the CCTV images that we have, and we've been circulating in the past couple of days, the officers who attended the scene have made a provisional identification. They believe it is the girl who witnessed the attack on DSu Scott. They believe she is Leila Ebaid.'

As Rula felt tears of shock and fury threatening, Tom Ireland went on. 'There's something for you to think about, Mr Drake,' he said. 'We'll be back.'

Chapter Thirty-Three

RIGOR

Wednesday

Paula spellchecked her report, saved it, and rolled back her chair. However you spun this, it was a failure. The coroner would rule an open verdict – accident, suicide or killing by person unknown – because she couldn't prove any of them. She had put the best gloss she could on it in her report, but the final recommendation to keep the case open but downgrade the investigation was an admission of defeat. It would go into cold cases and disappear. Already new cases were coming in, with claims for urgent action: a suspicious house fire with a woman badly injured, the disappearance of a vulnerable teenager, reports of an upswing in Rohypnol circulating the clubs. She couldn't justify giving priority to the mildly suspicious death of a man already in the borderlands between life and death.

But it irked her, not just because she didn't like to fail, but because she felt that the answer was only just out of reach. Someone was not telling her all they knew. She wanted to think that it was Gina Gray. It was unreasonable, she knew, but then Gina was an unreasonable woman.

Thoughts of Gina inevitably evoked thoughts of David, and of Rula. On an impulse, she picked up her phone and sent a text.

Stalled here, and moving on. You? Any good news please pass on. In need of cheer. xxx

She looked at her message. Were the three *x*s too girly? Well, to hell with it. She pressed *send.*

Rula's reply pinged in ten minutes later:

On river bank with body of our only poss witness. ETOD while only sus in our custody. Not great but we will get the fucker. Sorry about yours xxx

Paula smiled.

Chapter Thirty-Four

SIGNAL TRANSDUCTION

Wednesday

Coming out of the art room, Freda realised that for a whole hour she hadn't thought about the weekend, about death and suspicion, about the pictures that kept swirling around in her head. Instead they had been looking at actual pictures – at paintings – and planning the backdrops for the Christmas play. She thought *Little Women* was a brilliant choice. It riled the boys, of course, but there were always more girls than boys wanting to be in school plays, so why shouldn't they have a chance of decent parts? And it was a really good adaptation they were doing, one which didn't try to squeeze in *Good Wives* as well, like the film did. It went from Christmas to Christmas, just the one year, and Mr March came home at the end – not quite as tear-jerkingly as in *The Railway Children*, but certainly good enough for a few people to be fishing for tissues.

The set was easy too. The whole thing was set in the March sitting room, with episodes like Amy going through the ice recounted to Marmee, and the Aphra Behn theatre had agreed to hire out furniture at a cut rate. Where Freda and the other set creators came in was the backdrops. Mrs Wade had the brilliant idea of creating a window effect upstage, with pictures of the garden at different times of the year projected onto the back wall. Freda and the team were going to paint the pictures, and Mrs Wade had the idea that they should look like nineteenth century paintings. So they had been looking at American landscapes, and Freda had been given the plum job – absolutely the best. She was painting the garden in snow, for the first scene and again for the last. She almost danced down the corridor on her way to pick up her coat from the sixth form common room.

She expected to find the room empty – it was nearly five o'clock – but she walked in to the sound of water running, and found Faith washing up mugs at the sink in the corner.

'Hi,' Freda said. And then, when Faith didn't answer, 'If that's the job of the deputy head girl, remind me not to stand for office.'

Faith didn't turn to look at her, but scrubbed viciously at a stained mug. 'They are such slobs,' she said. 'Who do they think is going to wash up their stuff? They know the cleaners won't do it. All they do is complain to Mrs Mancini, and then she complains to Justin or me. And Justin's not going to wash up, is he? So it's down to me. Grrr!'

Now she turned to Freda, rubber-gloved, brandishing her washing-up brush.

Freda said, 'You look very professional. Are those the gloves we used at Stourly?'

Then she felt herself grow hot because it was crass to refer to the college in that casual way, but Faith seemed unfazed. She picked up the box of disposable gloves lying by the draining board.

'They are the very same,' she said. 'I thought it might encourage the girls at least, if they weren't going to spoil their lovely hands.'

Freda looked at her. 'Do you mean you pinched them?' she asked.

'I did. I thought Alice could spare them. There was a whole stack of them.'

'Well, that solves a minor mystery,' Freda said. 'I couldn't find them and had to start a new box when I was washing up.'

Then she felt herself blushing again, because that had been on the Sunday, only hours after they had found Faith's stepdad. Flustered, she went through to the lockers to get her coat, and as she put it on she realised that she wasn't feeling just embarrassed but uneasy. Something was causing little worms of dread to squirm in her stomach. Something wasn't right, and again she felt that dim sense that she knew something but it was just out of reach. Then she walked back through to the common room, saw Faith's laptop lying on a chair, and saw the picture that her mind had been refusing to show her.

She went to the window and looked out, then took a deep breath and went over to pick up a tea towel and start drying the mugs lined up on the draining board.

'So, have you sent your UCAS form in, finally?' she asked, quelling a treacherous wobble in her voice.

'Yup.' Faith put the last mug on the draining board and emptied the water from the washing-up bowl. Then she picked up another tea towel and joined Freda in drying the remaining mugs. They were very close, and Freda's hands were shaking. She thought it was quite likely that she would drop a mug.

'People do seem to make a big deal out of deciding their choices,' she said. 'Are you still putting Marlbury Uni as your first choice?'

Faith started arranging the dried mugs on the shelf above the sink, so that she had her back to Freda. 'Things are different now,' she said. 'I'm trying for Cambridge.'

Freda hung up her tea towel and went across the room to pick up her bag. The picture was quite clear now: the grey light of early Sunday morning, the bright screen of Faith's laptop, balanced on her knees in bed, Lisa's panicky banging on their door, the race downstairs. And then, later, when she had phoned 999, mechanically tidying their room, and closing down Faith's laptop, which was still showing her UCAS form, with Cambridge at the top.

'You were working on your form when Lisa came in on Sunday morning,' she said, making a show of checking the contents of her bag so that she didn't have to look at Faith. 'Had you been at it ever since you came back from your trip to the loo?'

'What trip to the loo?' Faith was, quite unnecessarily, rearranging the mugs.

'You remember,' Freda said, willing her now to turn round and look at her. 'You went to the loo in the night, and you came back and tripped over some shoes or something, and knocked something off the dressing table. You woke me up.'

'You must have been dreaming. I never need the loo in the night.'

'Then you'd been somewhere else,' Freda said. She was so angry now at the obvious lie that she decided to just come out with her suspicion. 'You went somewhere, and then you came back and changed your UCAS form. And that was the night the kitchen gloves went missing. Where had you been, Faith? How come you knew that you were going to be free now to try for Cambridge?'

Faith gave a hard, unconvincing hoot of laughter and disappeared into the locker room. Freda heard her opening her locker and wondered, for a wild moment, if she was going to come back with a knife – or even a syringe – in her hand. Had she still got the rubber gloves on? Freda adjusted her hold on the strap of her bag, ready to swing, but Faith came back with her coat on, empty-handed. She didn't need a weapon. Before Freda could think to raise her bag in self-defence, Faith strode across the room and slapped her hard across the face.

'Don't fucking Miss Marple me, Freda,' she hissed, 'thinking you can take after your fucking granny. Just drop it before you make an idiot of yourself.'

She swung away and walked out. Freda was left wiping away the tears that were pouring after the slap, but even through the tears she had noticed Faith's hands, without the gloves now. The nails were bitten down as though some rodent had been at them, and were ringed with crusted blood where the skin around them had been picked away.

Chapter Thirty-Five

REFRACTORY PERIOD

Thursday

'He's not going to talk,' Tom Ireland said, as he and Rula left the interview room and the door slammed behind them. Their third interrogation of Brian Drake. Fizzing with frustration herself, Rula felt that she was in the force field of Tom Ireland's anger as well, and was almost scared by it.

'You'd think the threat of two conspiracy charges would get him to crack,' she said.

'Why would it?' Tom Ireland challenged. 'If he gives us David's attacker and Leila Ebaid's killer – who may be one and the same person, but not necessarily, depending on the size of his operation – then it's in their interests to give him up – give us the whole shebang. Then the most expensive silk he can get isn't going to make the philanthropic support of asylum seekers angle work. So his only hope is that we're so incompetent that we won't find them, and at the moment it looks as though we are just that incompetent.'

He was striding so fast in his fury that Rula was almost running to keep up with him.

'I've been thinking,' she panted.

'And?'

'And given that Drake is an ex-cop, shouldn't we be thinking that the guys working for him might be ex-cops too – either sacked or pushed into going, like Drake? Especially if David had a hand in getting rid of them? And he's been doing his Saturday run for years. If the attack on him was planned, those guys would have known where to find him.'

Tom Ireland stopped dead, so that Rula almost cannoned into him.

'Why didn't we think of that?' he said.

'Because the Met is under threat, and we want to believe that there are only a few rotten apples?'

'The team won't like it, digging in the apple barrel – lots of maggots.'

And then Rula's phone rang. 'What do you want, Gina?' she said.

Chapter Thirty-Six

COVALENT BOND

Thursday

I really don't know why I am doing this. I am on a train, pootling from Stourly to Marlbury, to meet Ruth Curtis for coffee. Why? Or, rather, why not? There are several reasons why this is a bad idea. For a start, I am certain to be recognised, since we have agreed to meet on the university campus, where I used to work, and in the past few days my name and face have been all over the media. I am wearing sunglasses, and a hat I found in the Red Cross shop in Stourly, but I shall have to take them off once I'm indoors, and there will be nothing to stop people from bustling up with intrusive enquiries about David. Then there is the spurious reason I gave Ruth for wanting to meet. It is true that, as the days have gone by, and David has not rejoined the world, I have resolutely refused to countenance the idea that he will die, but have also grown ever more panicky about my future role as nurse, companion and ray of sunshine to a very badly damaged man. So it had crossed my mind that I might, at some point, talk to Ruth, who nursed one husband through a final illness, and was, apparently, ready and willing to do it again. But I wasn't thinking of face to face, where I couldn't disguise my panic. A phone call, possibly, or more probably an email. I wasn't hopeful about it, anyway. I know the answer, really. You have to be patient, unselfish and optimistic, while I am famously impatient, monumentally self-centred, and prone to pathological despair. However, this is the reason I have given to Ruth for wanting to meet, because I can't possibly tell her the real reason, which is that Freda believes that Ruth's daughter killed her stepfather.

I rang Ruth this morning to make this appointment after a sleepless night in which I tried to make sense of a hysterical phone call from Freda. I had never heard Freda like this before – not when she had been trapped in a cupboard by a man with a lethal weapon, not when her grandfather was found murdered in the bedroom next to hers. I kept telling her to talk to her mother, or to Ben, who could offer reassuring hugs and hot drinks, but she refused because her mother would *make a fuss*, disregarding the fact that she was making enough fuss for both of them.

What I made out, amid the tears and the *Oh my god* diversions, is that Freda seriously believes that Faith killed her stepfather with an overdose of insulin, because he would have stopped her from going to Cambridge. Now I do remember Ruth saying, when we met in Stourly, that Faith was going to stay at home and go to Marlbury, so that she could help her mother, but I can't believe that anyone was forcing her. Ruth doesn't seem like that sort of mother at all. And there was other stuff that Freda was obsessing about – rubber gloves and washing up, tripping over shoes and not going to the loo in the night – which I couldn't get a grip on. And then, finally, she said, *And she hit me. Across the face. Really hard. I'm getting a black eye.*

So then I was the one who panicked. If Freda is right, and Faith is a killer, and Faith knows that she knows, and has been violent to her already, and Freda won't tell her parents, then it has to be up to me. In the night, I thought that telling Paula would be the right thing, but Freda's evidence seems so flimsy – the more I tried to pin her down about it, the more tearful she got, shouting, *I just know!* And even the slap proves nothing – you can slap someone for thinking you're a murderer whether you are or not. So that was when I decided to talk to Ruth. If there is any chance that Faith killed her stepfather, Ruth will surely know. Just how I'm going to raise the subject I have no idea, but I have told Freda to make sure she is never alone with Faith today, and I have promised that I will sort things out.

On my walk to the university from Marlbury station, I test out possible opening strategies in my head, and realise, from the odd looks I get, that, along with the unnecessary dark glasses and the improbable hat, I am muttering to myself. This has got to stop.

I am no nearer an opening gambit when I walk into the campus café, where we have agreed to meet. Term hasn't started yet, so the place is eerily quiet, and I feel more exposed to being recognised and assailed. I am early, and Ruth is not here yet, so I hastily buy a cappuccino and find a table in the murkiest corner I can find. I don't buy cake. This is one of those few situations that can't be helped by cake.

Ruth arrives bang on time, as professionally dressed as usual but looking terrible. The last time I saw her, on the day of her husband's death, she was just looking pale and red-eyed, but now her face seems to have collapsed. She can't have lost pounds in four days, but that's what it looks like. *Haunted* is the word that comes into my mind.

She gets herself an espresso and comes to join me. After hellos, I have no idea what to say to her. I hoped that I would find inspiration when the moment came, but instead I feel in my head the kind of panicky nothingness that you get when, for a moment, you can't remember your next line on stage.

I am rescued by her asking the perfectly simple question, 'How are you?'

Why didn't I think of that? Or of an answer, if it comes to that?

'Oh, you know,' I say, vaguely and unsatisfactorily.

She doesn't ask a follow-up question, but I feel obliged to say something more.

'The hospital is tight-lipped about progress,' I say. And then in the most embarrassingly clumsy segue, 'As you are finding with the police, I imagine?'

She doesn't answer immediately, but gazes bleakly out of the nearest plate glass window, stirring her coffee, though she has put no sugar into it.

Eventually, she says, 'I think DI Powell is giving up. *Ongoing but rather more low-key* apparently describes the case now. But I still don't know when we can have the funeral.'

'That must be hard,' I say. And then, in a slightly less clumsy move, 'How is Faith coping?'

'I don't know,' she says, still not looking at me. 'She's not living at home.'

'Not at home?' I echo stupidly.

'She's staying with a school friend. She and I can't be together at the moment.'

This is interesting. I take a risk. 'Freda tells me that Faith is applying for Cambridge after all,' I say.

Now she does turn to look at me. 'She could always have done that,' she says. 'I would never have stopped her.'

'I'm sure you wouldn't.'

She leans forward. 'It was her decision to stay in Marlbury to help me with Hywel. I never asked her to. But I was asking too much of her all the same.'

'In what way?'

'Insisting that I would look after Hywel myself. It frightened Faith. After I nursed my first husband through his last illness, I had something of a breakdown. I was briefly sectioned for my own safety. I was a suicide risk.'

I am astonished. Even in her distressed state this morning, she seems perfectly sane.

'Faith was afraid of losing me. She had lost her father, and she was going to lose her stepfather, whom she did love, I think. She couldn't risk losing me too. So she was going to stay in Marlbury to look after me. And then -'

She stops, and I take a risk. 'And then she saw another way,' I say.

She doesn't answer directly, of course. She waits for a moment, and then she says, again, 'I asked too much of her. I didn't understand. I should have thought.'

And then she seems to realise that she has said too much. 'But you wanted to talk to me,' she says. 'You thought I might be able to give you some advice – because I have managed things so well myself, haven't I?'

She gives an odd, harsh laugh, and I think that it's not that difficult to imagine her as a psychiatric patient after all.

I say, 'I hoped you might help me to find the right mindset for looking after a sick partner – if I'm lucky, and I get the chance. I imagined that you had found it easy, because you were ready to do it again, but I realise I was stupid. It's never easy, is it?'

'No.' She hasn't touched her coffee, except to stir it. Now she swallows it in one go and stands up. 'Imagination,' she says. 'I think you have plenty of that. Imagine how things look from the other person's point of view. That's all.'

She looks as though she is about to go, but feels that I deserve more.

'You were very kind on Sunday,' she says. 'I'm sorry to have pressed you to talk to DI Powell. I hadn't had a chance to think things through to the obvious answer. I have thought about our cake lunch, and the waitress saying *You hate it*, and your little lecture about initial aspirates – one of the more bizarre moments of all this.'

I stare at her. '*Gotta hate hate,*' I say, as she stares at me. 'I have to – sorry – I must,' I say, as I rummage frantically for my phone. 'I knew it couldn't be…'

I locate the phone, and back away from her, scrolling for Rula's number. 'I hope everything – works out,' I say, as I press buttons and run outside.

Chapter Thirty-Seven

BIOINFORMATICS

Thursday

'What do you want, Gina?'

'Rula! Listen, I've just realised something. It wasn't *hate*.'

'What?'

'It wasn't *hate*.'

'What wasn't hate, Gina? I don't know what you're talking about.'

Rula rolled her eyes at Tom Ireland, who mouthed, '*David's Gina?*'

She nodded, and said, 'Can you slow down a bit, Gina, and tell me what this is about?'

'The last thing David said. I knew it couldn't be *hate*. Not David. And I've just realised, because of the waitress in the café – but that doesn't matter. The point is, when we're struggling to speak we hyperaspirate, so—'

'We do what?'

'Hyperaspirate. We push our breath out too hard, so we make '*h*' sounds before vowels which shouldn't be there.'

'So what do you think he was saying?'

'*Eight eight*, obviously!'

'I see.' Rula thought about what she could possibly say

next, and opted for simplicity. 'I have no idea how that helps us, Gina.'

'Oh, for heaven's sake! *Gotta eight eight.* Like you said, he was being a policeman, wasn't he? He was giving you information.'

'What kind of information would that be, then?'

'Well, I don't know, do I?' Gina's voice rose in exasperation. 'He'd seen the numbers – the end of a car number, maybe, or on a badge of some sort. Maybe his attacker was wearing a uniform of some sort, with a number on. He could even have been a police officer, have you thought of that? Right outside HQ. And if he had it in for David, he would have known about his early morning run. Now I think about it, I'm sure that's your way to go.'

Rula took a deep breath, and then said, all on the one breath, 'Well that's great thanks for sharing we'll certainly bear it in mind take care bye.'

She pocketed her phone and blew out another breath.

'What was that?' Tom Ireland asked.

Rula sat down and closed her eyes for a moment. 'I think she's losing it a bit,' she said, Gina's agitated voice still ringing in her head. 'I think it is literally driving her mad having the same message from the hospital day after day. She's got a thing about what the paramedic heard David say – or thought he heard him say. She was really upset that it was *hate, hate.* I think she was hoping his last words would be for her. She went on about 9/11, and everyone using their last phone calls to send messages of love. She didn't want to believe that David talked about hate. I think I may have complicated things because I said it was most likely that David was trying to give some information about his attacker. So now she's decided that he was saying *eight eight,* and that's the magic clue that's going to solve everything.'

Tom Ireland sat down too, in the only other chair in his office. 'Does she have any suggestions about what it might mean?' he asked.

'Oh yes. She started with a car number, but we know from CCTV that there were no cars around. Or someone wearing a number, which takes her to a uniform, which takes her to David being attacked by a police officer. We didn't get any further because I pulled the plug.'

Tom Ireland scratched his head, and Rula was taken aback to see that he wasn't immediately dismissing this.

'Let's unpack that a bit,' he said. 'She's right that we need to be looking at ourselves. The uniform with ID doesn't work if our man is the one seen by Mark Small at the station, and visible on CCTV with Leila Ebeid. That man is wearing a black T-shirt. So that doesn't work, and for the moment I can't see how *eight eight* helps us, but I've been unbelievably stupid in not realising that, of course, Brian Drake will have looked to other bent ex-cops like him when he's recruiting.'

'So DNA,' Rula said. 'Easy. We all have our DNA on record for elimination at a crime scene. It just depends how long that record is kept after someone leaves.'

'I think it's forever – for cold cases and appeals – contaminated evidence arguments. It ought to be, but there's no understanding the logic of the powers that be, and given our luck in this case, who knows? Can you get onto it?'

'I will. And if we're taking Gina seriously for the moment, there's another thought. That DNA under David's nails. Remember there was a trace of tattoo ink? Suppose *88* was a tattoo? It could be, couldn't it? A birthday, couldn't it? 8th August. Or 1988?'

She was puzzled to see Tom Ireland's face distort into a grimace of distaste. 'It's not a birthday, Rula,' he said. 'Don't you know what *88* is?'

'No?'

'You've never policed a demo where the National Front were out, then. The eighth letter of the alphabet is *H*. *HH* stands for—'

'*Heil Hitler*,' Rula said. She slumped in her chair. 'It's a Nazi code.'

'It's tenuous,' Tom Ireland said. '*If* David said *eight eight*; *if* he saw a tattoo. But I think it's worth getting onto Counter Intelligence. I'll bet they have a database of police officers with links to extremism. Our Home Secretary believes that too many police officers belong to lefty, Guardian-reading groups, but she's delusional. It's out on the right she needs to be looking.'

'I tell you what would be wonderful,' Rula said, sitting up and taking a deep breath. 'If, when we have our medicals, MOs make a note of people's tattoos.'

'Yeah, yeah,' Tom Ireland said, 'and if the records are still there, and there are a few pigs flying around the car park.'

'If you're contacting CI, I'm ringing our records office now,' Rula said. 'Better still, I'm going down there, and then we'll see.'

She got up, and then stopped. 'Just a thought, but if David saw a tattoo, wouldn't Mark Small have seen it? He seemed a pretty observant bloke.'

'The DNA shows that David and his attacker got close – probably had a struggle. It could have been under his T-shirt.'

'It could.'

She raced down the flights of stairs to the basement Records Office, where she found Jenna, who she regularly played squash with, on duty at the enquiries desk. Breathless, she said, 'Jen, my dear friend, you have to stop whatever you're doing and help me!'

'What's it worth?' Jenna asked, swinging her chair away from her computer screen.

'My shout for the drinks on Saturday.'

'You're on. What's the ask?'

'Two things. One, for how long do you keep fingerprint and DNA records for former officers? Two, do you keep medical records for ex-officers, and do you know if the MOs make a note of tattoos?'

Jenna gave her a long, assessing look. She knew exactly what this was about, Rula thought.

'It's a game of two halves, darling,' she said. 'Medical records are deleted as soon as someone leaves. Privacy laws. We're only entitled to have them while they are relevant to the officer's work – and then only with his/her permission. As for tattoos, I wouldn't know. I don't have access to those records. My guess would be only if the tattoo was a problem – infected or something. But we don't have them anyway. However, DNA and prints we do have – no problem. We keep them forever for cold cases being dug up, and legal appeals.'

'Great. Are they kept on the same database as serving officers?'

'No. They get moved. But there's no problem with access. You'll find them on the intranet.'

'Perfect. Thanks, Jenna.'

She had turned to go when Jenna asked, 'Were you looking for a particular tattoo?

'Very confidential, Jen. *Eight, eight.*'

'*Eight, eight.* What's that?'

'Eighth letter of the alphabet. Stands for HH. Stands for *Heil Hitler.*'

Jenna stared at her. 'Yuk!' she said.

Back in Tom Ireland's office, she found him at his computer.

'How did you get on with CI?' she asked.

'They'll do it, but they want a written request. I'm emailing it now. It took a while to get across to CI's finest on the phone that I couldn't get authorisation from my superintendent because it was the man who had put him in a coma who was the subject of our inquiry.'

'Counter unintelligence strikes again,' she said.

'How did you get on?' He swivelled his chair to look at her.

'Good news or bad first?' she asked.

'Let's have the bad.'

'Medical records are deleted as soon as someone leaves. Privacy rights kick in.'

'And the good?'

'The good is that DNA stays on record more or less forever, and we can access that database whenever we like.'

'Good. It's time to muster the troops. The incident room in fifteen minutes.'

'You're going to tell them all of it? The *eight eight* tattoo hunch?'

'Try not to call it a hunch, DI Bartosz. We have forensic evidence for the tattoo, and the word of a linguistic expert for *eight eight*. What was the fancy term she used? '

'*Hyperaspirate.*'

'There you go. They're desperate for something, and we've got nothing to offer them from interviewing Brian Drake.'

'I'll page them about the meeting. Someone might have seen the tattoo. You guys see each other in the showers at the gym, don't you?'

'If we go to the gym,' Tom Ireland said, patting the comfortable bulge above his belt.

'I had another thought about who might have seen the tattoo.'

'Oh yes?'

'The medical records have been deleted and we don't know that tattoos would be in them anyway – but the MOs will have seen people's tattoos. What's to stop us asking them – informally? I know one of them.'

'What's to stop us is patient confidentiality, DI Bartosz, and a doctor risking getting struck off.'

'But it's not medical, is it, a tattoo? I don't see how confidentiality—'

'Absolutely not! And we certainly couldn't reveal our source in court. Do not go there, Rula. I mean it.'

Downstairs in the incident room fifteen minutes later, the atmosphere was a sort of wary excitement, because, of course, the team would be expecting news that the morning's interrogation of Brian Drake had produced results. Tom Ireland needed to make their flimsy maybes sound convincing, and she wasn't sure he had it in him.

But he was a revelation – steady, cautious DCI Ireland spinning plates. Without actually stating that they had information from Brian Drake, he implied it:

'Given the evidence we have about a people-trafficking outfit run by a disaffected former officer, and that outfit's link to the abduction and murder of Leila Ebaid, seen on CCTV with our prime suspect, we are now looking urgently at other ex-officers, recruited by Brian Drake. So a priority now is to scan the DNA database for ex-officers, looking for a match with that taken from DSu Scott. That sample also contains traces of ink, identified as tattoo ink, and we have a lead on that too. A linguistics expert has been consulted about the last words DSu Scott spoke, as reported by one of the paramedics.'

Consulted! Rula thought, remembering Gina's babbling phone call.

'The words reported as *hate, hate* are more likely to have been *eight, eight.* There is something called, I believe, *hyper-aspirating.*' He glanced at Rula. 'If someone is finding it an effort to force words out, they are liable to produce an extra '*h*' sound. Taking that together with evidence of a tattoo which DSu Scott must have seen, since traces of it were under his nails, we believe that our suspect may have a tattoo of two figure eights.'

The room was very quiet. Tom Ireland looked around. 'Do we all know what a double eight tattoo means?' he asked.

Uneasy silence. One or two slight nods. Some people looked at the ground.

'Would anyone like to spell it out for us?' he asked. 'Just to be sure we all know?'

No reaction, and then Meera's hand went up.

'DS Javid?' Tom Ireland said.

'It is a recognised code for neo-Nazis. It stands for *Heil Hitler.*'

She said it without emotion, still the model pupil answering in class, Rula thought, and she automatically looked to the back corner of the room, where Wayne Cotton and his hangers-on sat, but there were no smirks there, no put-downs. Cotton had been pretty subdued, she thought, since he had blundered into that nail bar. Perhaps he was learning.

'Thank you, Meera. So our suspect may be a member of an extremist right-wing group, and I've put in a request to Counter Intelligence for anything they have on former police officers, though anything they have is unlikely to include their tattoos. So, I'm asking all of you to search your memories for any tattoos of that kind that you have seen on fellow officers. And in the meantime, volunteers for the DNA matching, please. Thank you.'

Looking at her watch, Rula guessed that most of the team would now be heading for the canteen, and she judged it better for them to talk among themselves. Besides, she wanted some space to clear her head and think about routes to identify that tattoo – if it existed. Did tattoo parlours keep records? They weren't obliged to, she felt sure – they weren't like dentists – and the ones who were prepared to do Nazi motifs were unlikely to.

She collected her coat and decided to take a walk, pick up a sandwich and a drinkable cup of coffee, and find a bench by the river. She stepped out into hazy sunshine and started to walk briskly in the direction of Costa Coffee. She wanted to feel positive, and if acting positive would do it, then she was in, but it was all, quite honestly, as shaky as hell.

And then she was conscious of running footsteps behind her. She swung round on the defensive, only to see Meera Javid sprinting towards her. Alert for trouble, she called, 'What's happened, Meera?'

Meera sped to a stop beside her – barely out of breath, Rula noticed, and said, 'I'm so sorry but I need to talk to you.'

'Now, Meera? I was just going to—'

'It is urgent, I think. About the tattoo.'

'Meera! I've told you. If you have information you must take it to DCI Ireland. He is the SIO. You must stop bringing things to me.'

Meera flushed. Rula could see the blood rush up under her olive skin.

'With this, I can't,' Meera said. 'It's not possible. I have to talk to you.'

Rula looked around. 'I'm going to bag that bench,' she said. 'You go to Costa Coffee and bring me back a ham and pickle sandwich and a black filter coffee. Here you are.' She fished in her wallet and produced a £20 note. 'Then we'll talk.'

While she waited for Meera, she looked out over the river and tried to focus on the moorhens rather than speculate pointlessly on what Meera had seen and why she couldn't talk to Tom Ireland. It was impossible, though. Her mind was spinning. If Meera had seen the *88* tattoos on someone, she would have to have seen that someone with few or no clothes on, which meant a relationship, surely, and she could see why Meera would be embarrassed to talk to Tom about that. But the idea of Meera in a relationship with any of the guys was impossible – let alone a neo-Nazi. So how could she have seen that tattoo?

Meera returned with a sandwich, coffee and change for her, and with a bottle of water for herself. Determined to be patient, Rula took the lid off her coffee to give it a chance to cool down, and let Meera take a swig from her bottle before she said, 'So are you going to tell me you've seen the *88* tattoos?'

Meera looked startled. 'Well, no, not that actual tattoo, but another one,' she said.

Oh for God's sake. How many more times? Every time, Rula thought. *Every time we think we're getting somewhere, and it's a mirage.*

She tore open her sandwich packet with unnecessary savagery and said, 'Another tattoo isn't exactly helpful, is it, Meera? Not if DSu Scott said *eight eight*? Or have you decided that he said something else?'

'No. No. But let me tell you.'

'Do.'

Meera set down her water bottle and put her hands in her lap, and looked down at them as she spoke.

'In the summer, I was working late one evening, and when I went out to the car park to get my bike, most of the cars had gone, and some of the guys were playing football – not a proper game, just a kick-around. They had made goals between two cars at either end. They were doing a lot of shouting and joking, and he – he asked if I wanted to join in, and they all hooted and whistled like they do, and I just put on my helmet and got ready to go. But then he must have kicked a goal, because he was running around waving his arms in the air, and he came over very close to me and he turned his back to me and

202

bent over and pulled down his shorts, and waggled his bare bottom at me, and he had tattoos – Her voice had clogged, and she cleared her throat. 'He had two swastikas tattooed on his bottom, one on each side.' Now she looked up at Rula. 'So I thought if he had those, why shouldn't he have *88* somewhere more visible, and I Googled before I came out to find you, and the most usual place for *88* is on the back, just below the neck. So if it was there, and DSu Scott grabbed hold of his T-shirt when they were struggling, he would have seen it.'

She was watching Rula with eyes bright with tears and excitement and Rula resisted an unprofessional urge to hug her – both to console and to congratulate – and went instead for the question to which she was pretty sure she knew the answer.

'You said *he*, Meera. Who was he?'

Meera stood up. 'You know,' she said.

Chapter Thirty-Eight

DIFFUSION

Thursday

Freda had spent the morning on high alert, avoiding Faith and surreptitiously switching on her phone between lessons, hoping one of her grandmother's exuberant, typo-strewn messages would arrive, with some inkling of what – if anything – she had achieved by talking to Faith's mother. The silence from Granny felt ominous, and by the end of the morning she was feeling that the best she could hope for was that the outcome of the conversation had been too complicated to be summed up in a text, and she might phone in the lunch break. Avoiding the common room, where Faith was likely to be, she took her packed lunch outside and started walking to the perimeter of the hockey pitch, attempting to eat a pitta bread that was threatening to ooze hummus all over her. If Granny was going to ring, she rather hoped that it would be after she had dealt with the hummus. In fact, it was not until she was making a dispirited return to the school building that her phone cheeped with a message. Freda read it:

Ruth knows and Faith knows that she knows.

Nothing for you to do. Leave it to them. AND DON'T WORRY!

xxx

This was all very well in its way, Freda thought, as she put her phone away, but now Ruth knew that Granny knew, and soon Faith would know, so what was going to happen?

Going to the common room to pick up her books for the afternoon, she found the room crammed with people, the entire sixth form gathered there.

'What's going on?' she asked Lisa, who was hovering near the door, looking pale.

'Mrs Mancini wants to see us all,' she said. 'I don't know why we couldn't have gone to the hall. I hate this squash.'

Before Freda could ask anything more, Mrs Mancini came in – looking, Freda thought, unusually ruffled. Hastily, she put up a hand for quiet, and spoke.

'I won't keep you long,' she said, 'but I thought it was important to speak to you all directly, before inaccurate rumours start circulating. You will all be aware, I think, that Faith Curtis, our Deputy Head Girl, suffered a loss at the weekend – the sudden death of her stepfather. Because of the circumstances of his death, the police have been involved, and this has been a stressful – not to say traumatic – time for Faith. She has bravely continued to attend school this week, and to carry on her duties, but it has been at a cost which we, perhaps, did not recognise. Faith's mother came to the school today to talk to me. She feels that for Faith simply to carry on as though nothing has happened would be seriously harmful to her mental health. She believes that a complete change of environment would be the best thing for Faith. Those of you who know Faith well will know that her mother comes from the USA. Her mother's sister has offered to have Faith to stay with her in Boston, and attend high school there. This will, of course, be an exciting experience for Faith, and a fresh start. Her mother is anxious that Faith should go as soon as she can, so that she misses as little of the new term as possible. Through her mother, Faith has US citizenship, so she will not have to wait for a visa. She plans to fly to the USA at the weekend. She has gone home with her mother now, and will not be in school again. I am sure she will be in touch with her friends in due course. We shall, of course, be sorry to lose her. Elections for a new deputy head girl will be held next week.'

Some hands started to go up, but Mrs Mancini held her own hands up to ward them off.

'I'm not taking questions,' she said. 'I have given you all the information I have. Off to afternoon classes, please.'

She doesn't believe it, Freda thought. *She doesn't believe a word of it. But she will never dare to guess the truth.*

Chapter Thirty-Nine

SOLVENT

Thursday

Rula herself ran the DNA database of current Met officers, and was unsurprised by the result. Meanwhile, Meera had sped off on her bike to Victoria station with a photo to show to ticket collector, Mark Small, and had come back looking triumphant.

It was agreed that the arrest should be kept low-key, so, towards the end of the afternoon, Rula got up from her place in the incident room, walked over to Wayne Cotton, and told him that DCI Ireland would like a word. His posse of admirers had made themselves scarce, she noticed. How much did they know? Well, that was for another day. The fall-out from this was going to be huge, but for the moment getting a confession out of Cotton was everything. He came quietly enough. Only the rapid blinking of his sharp little eyes betrayed any anxiety, though he must be anxious, Rula thought, knowing that they had interviewed Brian Drake. Unless he was confident that Drake wouldn't have talked.

In Tom Ireland's office, Rula made the arrest, on suspicion of people trafficking and of attempted murder. Wayne Cotton brazened it out. 'God,' he said, 'we are grasping at straws, aren't we?' Even when two uniforms arrived to cuff him and take him away, he managed a swagger as he departed, handcuffs and all.

'I thought you might ask him to show us his tattoos,' Rula said, when the door had closed.

'I'm saving that bit of theatre for later. It can only be corroborating evidence. We can't prove that what David said was *eight, eight*. A good brief would soon demolish that – and Mark Small's identification. The DNA is our key evidence. The rest will depend on us convincing Cotton that Brian Drake is ready to talk. We'll let him sweat for a bit while he thinks about his options.'

'I was thinking about the interview,' Rula said. 'How would you feel about taking Meera Javid in with you?'

'As well as you?'

'Instead of me. I can watch from the obs room.'

Tom Ireland gave a soft whistle. 'Do you think she can handle it?' he asked. 'It's going to be ugly. He'll be a dirty fighter, and he'll go for her as the soft target.'

'I think she has endured more from him than any of us knew. She's coped so far, and I think she deserves to be in at the kill. Can we at least ask her if she wants it?'

'Ask her, but warn her that she'll have to tough it out.'

'I will.'

'You don't mind missing out?'

'I'll take it as a masterclass.'

'Flattery will take you a long way, DI Bartosz.'

He smiled, and Rula thought it was the first time she had seen him smile in the past five days.

Meera responded to the invitation to join the interrogation with a tightening of her lips and a glint of tears. 'Thank you,' she said.

'DCI Ireland thinks he will turn ugly,' Rula warned.

'But I shan't be on my own, shall I?' Meera said.

Rula wondered wat had happened in the past when she had been on her own. A hot surge of guilt hit her. She had known – or guessed – the sort of harassment Meera got when there was no-one there to protect her, but she had had some of it herself and she'd let herself give in to the macho culture – to the *think you're tough enough to be a cop then prove it* mentality, and she had never allowed herself to think how much worse it must have been for Meera.

'No, you won't be on your own,' she said. 'Enjoy it!'

She took herself to the observation room and looked down, through the one-way glass, at the interview room below. Wayne Cotton was in the room already, with two uniformed officers at the door. He was lounging in his chair – he would know that he could be observed, of course.

When Tom Ireland and Meera entered the room, he sat up and jabbed a finger at Meera.

'What's the Paki doing here?' he demanded. 'Don't I rate a proper cop?'

Tom Ireland said, 'I am about to start the recording, DC Cotton. I'm sure I don't need to remind you that anything you say may be reported in court. You want to be careful about giving offence.'

'Plenty of jurors'd be cheering for me – you'd be surprised. Anyway, it's not going to court, is it? I'm innocent and you've got nothing on me.'

Tom Ireland turned on the recorder. 'Interview of Wayne Colin Cotton commencing at eighteen ten, interview room one. Officers present, DCI Thomas Ireland and DS Meera Javid. Wayne Cotton has waived his right to have a solicitor present.'

He sat down. 'Let's start with that. No solicitor. Why have you elected not to have a lawyer here?'

Wayne Cotton leaned back in his chair and crossed his legs. *Overacting*, Rula thought.

'I told you, I'm innocent. And if I did want a lawyer, I wouldn't use a poxy duty solicitor – some wet-behind-the ears work experience guy – or bint, even worse. If I think I need a brief, I'll get the best going – no expense spared.'

You think Brian Drake will pay, don't you? Rula thought.

'Well, if you change your mind, you still have the right to ask for a solicitor. Let's move on.' Tom Ireland turned to Meera. 'DS Javid, will you show Mr Cotton the DNA profile taken from our records of current Met officers?'

Meera opened a folder in front of her and pushed a sheet of paper across. Rula was glad to see her look him straight in the eye as she did so.

'For the recording,' Tom Ireland said, 'DC Javid is passing Mr Cotton a printout of his own DNA profile. She will now show him a second printout – this one is of the DNA found on Detective Superintendent David Scott immediately after the assault made on him on 18th September.'

Meera pushed a second sheet across, still keeping her eyes on Cotton. He glanced briefly at the two sheets and then pushed them back.

'Contamination,' he said. 'DSu Scott and I work together – we rub shoulders. Why shouldn't he have some specks of my DNA on him?'

'It was first thing in the morning,' Meera said quietly. 'DSu Scott hadn't yet been into the station. And he wasn't wearing work clothes – he was in his running clothes. And your DNA was under his fingernails. He had touched you. Probably scratched you,'

Cotton smiled – something between a smirk and a leer. 'We are very close, Dave and me,' he said. Then he turned to Tom Ireland. 'Are you going to let her just chip in whenever she feels like it? Can't you keep the bitch under control?'

Rula didn't look at Meera, but she watched a flush of anger spread up into Tom Ireland's face.

'DS Javid and I are conducting this interview jointly. DS Javid will ask you questions without the need for my permission. And I will warn you again about the language you use in this interview, bearing in mind that any part of it may be played in court.'

'And I'm warning you that this isn't going to court, and when you have to drop all charges you'll need to find a very safe safe house for the Paki because we'll be after her.'

'Threatening a police officer is an offence, as you know.'

'And she offends me just by being here.'

Tom Ireland didn't look at Meera, but Rula did, and saw perfect composure, with just a tightness around her mouth as any sort of giveaway.

Tom Ireland said, 'Moving on. When you were searched after your arrest, you were found to have a tattoo of two number eights at the base of your neck. Do you acknowledge that you have those tattoos?'

'I certainly do. Do you want to see them? Give the Pa – sorry, DS Javid – a thrill?'

Slowly, he started to unbutton his shirt. 'For the recording,' he said, 'DC Cotton is doing a striptease.'

'You can stop that,' Tom Ireland said, 'or you'll be restrained. We have photographs of the tattoos and that's enough.'

He glanced at Meera, who opened the folder in front of her and took out several photos.

'For the recording, DS Javid is showing Mr Cotton photos of a tattoo of two figure eights, placed either side of the spine at the base of a neck. Do you recognise these tattoos as yours, Mr Cotton?'

'Yeah. Nice, aren't they? Are you sure DS Javid wouldn't like to see them in the flesh?'

'More to the point, can you explain to us why you didn't mention these tattoos at the team meeting this morning, when the possibility was raised that what the paramedic who attended to DSu Scott heard him say was *eight, eight,* and he might have been identifying his attacker by a tattoo he had seen on him?'

'You know why. Teacher's pet here told us all about it this morning. My tattoos signify my political views, and all you bleeding-heart lefties would be screaming *banned organisation* at me.'

'Are you a member of a banned organisation?'

'As it happens, no. But I have friends who share my views, and I keep my tattoos covered except when I'm with them.'

The man who attacked DSu Scott was wearing a high-necked black T-shirt. In a struggle, DSu Scott could very easily have grabbed at the back of the T-shirt, revealing the tattoo and taking fragments of tattooed skin away.'

'But you can't prove that happened, and you can't prove the man was me. You got any idea how many tattooed men there are in London?'

'As a matter of fact, you've been identified. The ticket collector at Victoria station that morning, Mark Small, has identified you, from a photo, as the man who accompanied Leila Ebeid off a train from Dover, and Leila Ebeid is the only person whose face is seen on CCTV at the spot where the attack took place, and her DNA was found on DSu Scott, as well as yours. The man who was with her kept his face away from the camera, as if he knew where they were. Who knows better where the cameras are outside Met HQ than someone who works there?'

'You won't make Mr Tiny's identification stick. The description he gave was nothing – 'specially with the wraparound shades.'

'Wraparound shades?'

'Yeah, the guy he saw was wearing wraparound shades, wasn't he?'

Meera leafed rapidly through the papers in her folder; Tom Ireland sat still, watching Cotton; Cotton started babbling.

'Well, I thought he said he was wearing wraparounds, but I might have—'

'Ah, here we are.' Tom Ireland took a sheet from Meera, scanned it rapidly, and passed it to Cotton. 'I'm passing a copy of Mr Mark Small's statement in which he describes the couple he saw, and I am asking Mr Cotton to show me where there is any mention of the man's dark glasses being of the wraparound variety.'

Wayne Cotton was sweating, Rula could see. He scanned the paper and then pushed it back. 'Must have imagined it,' he muttered.

Tom Ireland leant forward, his arms on the table between them, and said, 'But you own a pair of wraparounds, don't you, Wayne? They're in the list of the contents of your pockets when you were arrested. Now, I'm going to give you a scenario, and then you can tell me how close I am to the truth. This is how I see it: you've been working for Brian Drake's little empire, bringing girls into the country – girls who who've lost their families on the journey to find asylum, girls whose families are so desperate that they've set their daughters off on the asylum trail as unaccompanied children, or girls who just want a chance of a better life. One of your jobs is to pick them up out of the water when they land on the coast, and bring them to London, where you put them in the kind of rat hole we found under the nail bar you led us to. That's just temporary, of course – it's one of Drake's brothels they're really destined for. How am I doing so far?'

Cotton was still shaken by his blunder over the shades, Rula could see, but he managed some of his old swagger, leaning back in his chair in an attempt to look relaxed.

'You've been in this job too long, DCI Ireland. It's sent you doolally,' he drawled.

'Maybe, but let's carry on. Last Saturday, you picked a girl up from Dover. Maybe it's just a weekend job for you, is it, seeing as you are supposed to be doing a full-time job here? The girl was Leila Ebeid, from Syria. She was only fifteen, but I expect Drake's clients like them young. You brought her to London on the train. I wonder why not by car. Maybe they vomit in a car, do they? And get seawater on the upholstery? Or maybe they're less suspicious than they would be if they were bundled into a car. It was more of a risk using the train, but it was very early on a Saturday morning, hardly anyone around. Unluckily for you, though, it was quiet enough at Victoria for the ticket collector to notice the two of you, and to think what an odd couple you made. And he noticed a smell that he couldn't identify at first, until he realised that it was the smell of seawater. An observant man, Mark Small, an excellent witness. All credit to DS Javid for finding him.'

'Go on, Tom, rub it in,' Rula muttered.

'So,' Tom Ireland went on, 'you bring her up to Victoria, and then you walk her along the Embankment, past Met HQ, and on the face of it that's a puzzle, because it's a long walk to that nail bar where she ended up – much easier to take the tube. So, either you were taking her somewhere near here first, or you had a special reason for bringing her past here. My guess is that was it – it made you feel like a big guy to bring her along here right under our noses. Did you know DSu Scott would be doing his Saturday morning run? Was that a bonus? Or maybe that was the whole point – to bring her here and see you stab a police officer outside a police station and walk away. Enough to terrify her into not trying to get away, and to settle your grudge with DSu Scott. Because he had the measure of you, didn't he? And he was out to get you just like he got Brian Drake?'

Wayne Cotton laughed, and then laughed again,

because the first laugh had sounded so unconvincing, even to him.

'This is such bullshit,' he said. 'You got no proof of any of it. It's all in your sick little mind.'

Tom Ireland just shook his head, but Meera spoke.

'You forget that we have Brian Drake – your boss – in custody. He is a very useful informant.'

Cotton smirked. 'You won't hold him, and he won't talk,' he said.

Meera almost mirrored the smirk, Rula thought, as she said, 'Well, we will hold him. He'll be in the magistrates' court tomorrow, and we'll oppose bail.'

'We're including a conspiracy to murder charge, along with several others, so there's no chance that a magistrate will grant bail.'

'What d'you mean, murder? Scott's alive, isn't he? Anyway, Brian didn't – you won't hold him. You don't know – he's got—'

'Friends in high places, has he?' Tom Ireland chipped in. 'Is that what he told you? Plays golf with the CC, does he? He took you for a mug, Wayne. He's just a bent ex-cop with a nasty little line in people trafficking. DS Javid saw him clearing his stuff out from that nail bar after you led us to it. If that was the nerve centre of his criminal empire, we're not impressed.'

'And why did you lead us there?' Meera asked, hardly able to hide how much she was enjoying herself. 'If you hadn't made up that story about going to search the place and "losing" Leila Ebeid, we'd probably never have found it. What was that about?'

'Wanted to put you off the scent,' Wayne Cotton growled, looking at Tom Ireland, not at Meera. 'You were sending us round the nail bars a second time, and there was a chance one of the girls would talk. I thought if I told you the girl had bolted from there you'd leave it alone.'

'She had a name – *the girl*,' Meera said furiously. 'She was Leila Ebeid, aged just fifteen, from Syria – which you're probably too ignorant to know has been wrecked by a war. She was a person with a family and a dream of a future.'

'Don't lose it, Meera,' Rula whispered.

Tom Ireland came in. 'The plan didn't work, Wayne, and Brian Drake is seriously pissed off with you.'

'So pissed off he'll tell us everything. Because it's not just the trafficking and the attack on a police officer, is it?' Meera said. 'You killed Leila Ebaid. Because you knew we would find her and she would talk. We know Brian Drake didn't kill her, because we had him in custody that night, but he had good reason to want her silenced. Maybe it was all your own idea to kill her, trying to make up for putting us on her trail, but Drake needed her silenced too, and you worked for him. We can make a very convincing case for conspiracy. Drake knows that, and he knows his only chance is to hand you over to us.'

'All nicely gift-wrapped,' Tom Ireland said. 'So if you want to get out of jail before you're a very old man, I'd advise you to tell us everything and plead guilty, and hope a nice old judge will take that into account.'

Wayne Cotton's body language didn't change, except that from her vantage point, Rula could see his hands tighten into fists under the table.

'He can't – about the girl – he didn't know,' he started, and then faltered to a stop.

How the hell did you get to be a detective, you brainless lump? Rula's internal commentator enquired.

'So why don't you tell us your story, Wayne, before we decide to believe him?'

There was a moment, and then Cotton leant forward and, avoiding Meera, looked earnestly into Tom's face. 'Look,' he said, 'it wasn't meant to happen with DSu Scott. It was all an accident. The girl's fault. Yes, I admit I picked her up in

216

Dover, but like Brian says, we're helping these girls. What was a girl like that going to do on her own. I was giving her protection.'

'Protection?' Meera asked quietly. 'What were you protecting her from?'

Tom Ireland put a warning hand on her arm. He wanted Cotton to keep going with his story.

'Yeah, protection,' Cotton spat. 'Food, clothes, shelter. Better than living on the street.'

'Go on,' Tom said.

'So I brought her up here, and yes, it was a bit of a laugh to walk her right past here. She was getting stroppy by this time. She came quiet enough in Dover, but then Mr Tiny at Victoria said something to her, and she started babbling. I couldn't understand a word of it but she looked like she was going to try a runner. So that was why I didn't want to take her on the tube, and I thought if I took her past HQ and told her I was a policeman, she'd see that she wasn't going to help herself by making a fuss, and she'd do as she was told.'

He stopped and stared down at the table. 'Silly bitch,' he said.

'Silly?'

'It was bad luck.' A whiny tone had come into Cotton's voice. 'I didn't know about Scott's Saturday run, I swear. First thing Saturday morning – that's a time I don't usually see. But he comes running along just at the wrong moment. The girl—'

'Leila,' Meera interrupted quietly.

'LEILA!' Cotton snarled back at her. 'She'd seen the sign outside HQ, and they all know what *POLICE* means, even if they don't know anything else. I had a had hold of her arm but she started to struggle, and then she saw Scott come along and turn to go inside, and she started to shout. I had to get her round the neck to shut her up.'

'What did DSu Scott do?'

'Well, he turns round and comes back, doesn't he? Stupid bastard. If he'd just blanked her it would all have been all right. But he's got to be a fucking hero, hasn't he? It wasn't my fault. It was self-defence. He comes at me, I try to run, he grabs me by the throat – he's stronger than you'd think for a desk jockey – I think he's going to strangle me, so I reach for my knife.'

Rula watched him spread his arms out in a sort of crazy appeal.

'It was self-defence,' he said.

There was a silence, then Tom Ireland said quietly, 'Three things. One, self-defence when apprehended by a police officer is known as resisting arrest; two, carrying an offensive weapon is a crime; three, you didn't just stab DSu Scott, you kicked him repeatedly in the head. He was on the ground, posing no threat to you.'

'I never!' Wayne Cotton protested. 'I made a run for it with the girl. It was someone else did that.'

'Someone else who is magically invisible on CCTV?' Meera asked. 'Or perhaps it was one of the officers who came to his aid? Or one of the paramedics having a bad day?'

'We'll soon know, anyway,' Tom Ireland said. 'The kicks to DSu Scott's head were so hard they left imprints of shoes or boots. The forensic team took photographs of them, and they'll be able to compare them with the footwear retrieved in a search of your flat this afternoon. They'll want the shoes you're wearing at the moment too, of course.'

He stood up. 'You can take him back,' he said to the officers on the door. 'Make sure those shoes go to the lab.'

As he and Meera left the room, Wayne Cotton turned for a last appeal. 'I didn't mean to,' he whined. 'It wasn't my fault.'

Rula ran down the stairs to meet Tom and Meera. Meera was almost dancing down the corridor.

'*Bang to rights*,' Rula said. 'Was that true about the footprints?'

'Well, the prints aren't that clear,' Tom Ireland said, 'but it's a possibility.'

'We never lied to him,' Meera said. 'You heard that.'

Rula laughed. 'No, you just relied on him being stupid. You never said that Brian Drake had spilt the beans on him. You just said he was pissed off with him, and that was the obvious thing for him to do to save his own skin. Cotton's too dim to spot the difference.'

'Cotton had put all his eggs in Drake's basket – believed his guff about friends in high places. Once we exploded that, I was pretty sure we'd get a confession of sorts.'

Meera said, 'Spilt beans and exploding eggs – sounds like his prison breakfast.'

Rula laughed, and found that she had tears in her eyes. It was the first time she had ever heard Meera make a joke.

'I had another thought while I was watching you,' she said. 'You know the paramedic thought David said, *Gotta hate, hate*, well I think it might not have been *gotta*. What he said could have been *Cotton*. Wouldn't that be David? His last conscious breaths, and he gives us the name and the identifying marks. There's no-one like him.'

Chapter Forty

SIGNAL TRANSDUCTION

Thursday

Rula has phoned me, and I am stomping round Stourly village in the drizzly dusk because I am too angry to sit in my room, or even in the haven of the café. As I stomp. I am muttering to myself, and – as is habitual these days – people are crossing the road to avoid me.

I am becoming The Mad Woman of Stourly, but I don't care. I am furious – furious with the Met for its incompetence and corruption, furious with the evil bastard they have been harbouring in their ranks, furious with the wretched girl who let herself be used by the evil bastard, and furious with David for being stupidly brave.

I feel as though I am going to go on walking and muttering until I fall down from exhaustion, but I am stopped in my tracks by another phone call.

'Yes,' I bark.

'Mrs Gray?' an unknown voice asks.

'Yes.'

'This is Staff Nurse Mayhew. I am calling about David Scott. We think you will want to come in.'

Come in? Of course I want to come in.

'I'll be there,' I say. 'I'm leaving now.'

And without going back to my room for anything, I turn and start running for the station.

Some kind of benign power seems to be looking out for me because I find a train about to leave the station, and I fling myself onto it. Then, as we are moving off, I panic that I might be being shunted into a siding, because the carriage I am in is empty. Reason should tell me that it is rush hour time, and commuters will be travelling out of London, not into it, but rationality is beyond me. I push my way out of the carriage and stagger down the train until I find a startled elderly man, sitting quietly with a newspaper, and demand to know if this train is going to London. He blinks at me and says he is getting off at the next stop, but he believes the train goes on to London. Can I trust him? The train is picking up speed now, so at least we're not heading for a siding. I sit down reluctantly, and then I see it – an electronic strip, like a message written on the sky by angels, telling me the names of all the stations we shall be stopping at, and ending with London Victoria. I give a little *yip* of relief, which further startles my fellow passenger, and which I try to turn into a cough. I really must settle down.

It may seem ridiculous, but it is not until I have paid the ticket collector and my fellow passenger has got off that I start to think about what lies ahead. And I realise that I have no idea. I am so stupid. These last days, every time I have spoken to anyone in the ICU I have asked when I can come in and see David, I have been fobbed off: *He's not ready; In a few days; We'll let you know,* and – most cuttingly – *We only allow very close relatives at this stage.* So, when the nurse rang and told me I could come, I assumed that meant an improvement, that David was fit to see me. Only now it hits me that it could mean the opposite. I try to dredge up exactly what she said. I think it was, *'We think you will want to come in'*, and linguistics expert though I am, I can't tell whether that means that David is dying.

I am glad I have the carriage to myself, because tears are running down my face. I stare blindly out of the window and think how stupid I have been, worrying about managing a disabled David. Faced with the real prospect of losing him, I know I want him with me in any state at all, and as terror grips me, I know something else: if David is dying, he will die with a lie between us – the lie I told by omission when I protected Irina and the other young women and let them go free after they murdered Ekrem Yilmaz. I have lived in bad faith with David for the past fifteen years, and it has bedevilled everything. It is a reason why I didn't marry him. Oddly, I see, it is the reason why I can't trust him. Untrustworthy myself, how can I?

As we approach Victoria, I try to pull myself together. I have run out of tissues, so I give my face a final wipe on my sleeve, and I put on the lipstick I find in the bottom of my bag. It turns out to be quite red, but perhaps it will distract from the red eyes.

It is still rush hour in London, so I don't risk a panic attack on the tube, but stand in the queue for taxis, where I am both desperate to move forward and equally desperate to stay put.

Most people walking the hospital corridors manage to look quite normal and unconcerned, as if the drama, death and despair happening behind closed doors were nothing to do with them. I know I look too distraught, and I feel the looks I get are more of disapproval than pity – I am letting the side down.

It takes me forever to find the ICU. I follow signs and get abandoned, I retrace my steps, I accost passing staff, and eventually I am there. I am admitted by a nurse, and when I say David's name I watch her face intently for clues, but it remains professionally blank. She just leads me through a small ward, where there are more machines than people, each with its barrage of beeps and lights. At the end of the ward is a door, which she opens, and then stands aside.

'In here,' she says.

EPILOGUE

FOUR LUNCHES

ONE
SEPTEMBER

Paula sat at a corner table, close enough to the log fire to appreciate its comfort but distant enough not to roast. *Sunday lunch in country pub?* she had texted to Rula. *You won't find one of those in Croydon.* Her excuse for the invitation had been *congratulations and commiserations* because, although Rula would be relieved at getting their man, finding that he was one of their own would have been a really bitter pill. And the media had gone in with all barrels. The Met was *broken, systemically corrupt, a branch of London's criminal community* – not to mention the inevitable *not fit for purpose.* She thought of the bizarre evening they had spent with Bridget, spinning their fantasy about Direnç Yilmaz as the perp in both their cases. They were wrong about both, and neither case had resolved well.

The door opened, and Rula walked in. She stopped, looking round uncertainly, then saw Paula stand up and wave. Meeting, they hesitated for a moment, then moved in for a slightly awkward hug.

'This is a new experience,' Rula said, 'and I can do with it.' She was looking good in a leaf-green sweater and jeans, and with her auburn curls released from the work day elastic band that had restrained them the last time they met. Her face showed the strain of the last few days, though – tension round her eyes and in the set of her mouth.

'Tough time?' Paula asked.

'You could say.'

'But you got him.'

'Yes!' Rula gave a growl of frustration. 'We got him. You'd think from the media coverage that we didn't do anything right. OK, they're entitled to be shocked at the corruption – we're shocked too – and they can go on about *systemic failures*, we know about those – but they barely mention that we broke a trafficking ring and rescued fifteen girls and women from brothels and night clubs – and they say nothing about David's sacrifice.' She rummaged in her shoulder bag for a tissue, and, not finding one, picked up her napkin and wiped her eyes.

'How is Gina coping? Do you know?'

'She's – it's a hard time for her. She's angry too. She didn't want to talk to me.'

They were silent. Then Paula said, 'So let's concentrate on the positive. You smashed the traffickers and you've cut out some rot. I want to drink to that.' She picked up her glass. 'What would you like to drink? Or do you want to have a look at the menu first? I'm drinking this low alcohol cider. It's not the best drink in the world, but it will go with the pork and apple sauce I'm having – and I'll be safe to drive home.'

Rula picked up her menu. 'I won't have pork,' she said, 'because my mum makes pork nearly every Sunday. Only she doesn't make it with roast potatoes and apple sauce – she makes dumplings and pickled red cabbage. I'd like beef, because I like Yorkshire pudding.'

'They do Yorkshire pud with all the roasts here. I think most pubs do now.'

'Ah, but I'm traditional,' Rula said. 'I'll try the cider, though.'

When they had given their orders and Rula had her cider, they clinked glasses, and Paula said, 'Congratulations, anyway, however the media choose to spin it. And well done your DS Javid. She sounds impressive.'

'She is. Bright and dogged. And she puts up with so much shit. If she can stand it, she could go a long way.'

'And how about you?' Paula asked. 'Do you want to move up to the dizzy heights of DCI?'

'I wasn't sure that I did, but I was really pissed off when Tom Ireland took the case off me, so I guess I do like being in charge.'

And then, by mutual consent, they stopped talking work. They enjoyed their lunch, swapped holiday stories, and Rula talked entertainingly and affectionately about her Polish family. It was only as they were leaving that Paula brought up work again. As they walked to their cars, Rula said how good it had been to get out of London, and that gave Paula the opening she had been hoping for.

'You know,' she said, 'putting aside the media hype, the Met is a pretty toxic place at the moment, isn't it – especially for women. It's a lot better down here. I had a hard time when I started, but nobody messes with me now. You could think of transferring. You still wouldn't be that far from your family.'

'And I could breathe fresh air, and have a dog, and take you out for Sunday lunch?'

'As often as you like,' Paula said.

TWO
OCTOBER

Freda had an arrangement to have lunch with her father. That is to say, her biological father – not Ben, who was her real father in every sense except the biological. The words *biological father* always made Freda want to giggle, because they conjured an image of eager little sperm swimming along. But they were better than the other words she had for him, which were *The Rapist*. Because, although her mother insisted that it was her fault – that she had *been stupid* – Freda and her friends agreed that what had happened had been a sort of date rape. Her mum didn't like talking about it, so Freda didn't know much, but what she did know was that Mum had been eighteen, just starting at university, and he had been older. She had gone to Oxford with a debating team, for a competition, he had got her drunk, and Freda had been the result. What was amazing, of course, was that Mum had decided to have her, when it would have been easy to have an abortion. When she asked her, Mum said, 'I thought I had to take responsibility, that you can't just pretend mistakes didn't happen. And then you turned out to be the sweetest thing in my life.'

Freda had asked why she hadn't told The Rapist about her, and Mum said that if he had ever bothered to contact her, she would have done, but he never did. And that would have been the end of it, except that it turned out that he knew Auntie Annie. They were both lawyers in the same chambers in London, before Auntie Annie moved to Scotland. Mum had recognised his name – the sort of name you didn't forget. Lyle Fenton, he was called, which sounded like a fake name to Freda. Privately, when she wasn't calling him The Rapist, she liked to anagrammatise him as Lenny Lofet, which took the poshness out of him.

So, why was she meeting him for lunch? She wasn't sure, except that she had told herself that when she was sixteen she would contact him. She couldn't help being curious about him, and she thought he might have grown up and improved. You had to give people a chance.

So here she was, sitting in a smart gastropub near his Gray's Inn chambers, and he was late. She felt conspicuous, sitting alone at a table, but she would have felt worse if Ben hadn't been sitting at the bar. His being there was the result of long and anxious conversations with Mum. She – with good reason – didn't trust Lyle Fenton. *Who invites a sixteen-year-old to lunch in a pub*, she demanded. *Supposing he didn't turn up? Supposing he upset her? Supposing he took her somewhere and then abandoned her, leaving her to find her own way back to St Pancras?* And then, in the end, Ben came up with a proposal. He needed to go to Boosey and Hawkes, he said, on a hunt for some obscure sheet music, so he could go up to London with Freda, see her safely linked up with Lyle Fenton, go off on his errand, and come back for her. Any problems, she could phone him, and he would come to her rescue. The cover story was almost convincing, though Freda and her mum both knew that he could almost certainly find what he wanted in the very good music shop in Marlbury, or on the Boosey and Hawkes website.

So here he was now, watching over her, and here was Lyle Fenton, coming into the pub and approaching her table. She stood up, uncertain what else to do. She hoped very much that he wouldn't try to hug her. He didn't. He just said, 'Freda,' and sat down.

Freda glanced over to where Ben was sitting. He got up and came over, stretching out his hand to Lyle Fenton in his easy, Italian way.

'Ben Biaggi,' he said, 'Freda's stepfather. Good to meet you. I'm just here as Freda's travelling companion. I've got some things to do, but I'll be back in an hour. Is that all right, Freda?'

She nodded, wanting suddenly to cry. He kissed the top of her head, gave her shoulder a reassuring squeeze, and was gone. Freda felt for her phone in her pocket, like a talisman.

'So, have you looked at the menu?' Lyle Fenton asked.

She supposed he was as nervous as she was. She had looked at the menu. She had had plenty of time since he was late – he hadn't apologised for that, so it was going in her mental debit column. On the credit side, he was good-looking, with a good haircut and cool clothes. She couldn't see anything of herself in him, except for his light hazel eyes. For some reason, she was glad about that.

'I'd like *pasta alla Norma*, please,' she said.

She was pleased with her choice: it was a proper Italian dish – Ben's mother made it – and it was made with penne, so there would be no embarrassing wrestling with spaghetti or linguine.

He said, 'Vegetarian, are you?' and didn't wait for an answer. 'I hope you don't object to my having meat.'

'As long as it isn't veal,' she said, and felt rather brave.

They ordered, the waiter brought drinks, he gestured vaguely with his wine glass, and said, 'Good to meet you,' and then he started on what Freda thought must have been a prepared list of questions. It was a bit like she imagined a job interview would be, except you didn't' know what the job was.

He started with school, of course: *had she done GCSEs? What A levels was she doing? What did she plan to do with them?* When she said she was thinking of art college and a career in set or costume design, he said an odd thing: 'Sounds like a pretty insecure sort of career. Lawyers aren't all rich, you know. People think we're all fat cats, but it's not true.'

Freda chewed on a mouthful of pasta and tried to see the connection between set design being insecure and lawyers not all being rich. Then she saw it. *He thinks I've made contact with him because I want money from him.*

He hadn't finished. 'And I don't suppose your parents have any money. Both teachers, aren't they?'

Freda finished her mouthful, put her fork down, and took a swig of her water. 'We have quite enough money,' she said. 'My mother is head of the arts faculty in a big school, and Ben is a brilliant musician, as well as a teacher.'

He looked at her. His face had an odd way of having no expression on it. 'Well, good,' he said.

As they finished their main courses – he was eating something with meatballs – she thought it was her turn to ask him a few questions. She didn't ask about his private life, but she asked if he liked living in London – *expensive*, was the answer – and if he went to the theatre much – also *expensive*. He volunteered that he liked to *play a bit of squash*, and that was it. Freda took the opportunity, when he was looking round at the other tables, which he did quite a lot, to get her phone out and check the time. *An hour*, Ben had said, and they had been here for forty-five minutes. She could manage another fifteen minutes, couldn't she?

It was a long fifteen minutes, not helped by the fact that Lenny Lofet, as she had definitely decided to think of him now, asked her if she wanted pudding in such a discouraging way that it gave her no option but to refuse. She was tempted to say, *too expensive*, but restrained herself. He checked his watch, without bothering to be surreptitious, and returned to his checklist of questions, asking about hobbies and interests but failing on supplementary questions.

For once in his life, Ben was early, coming in with his big smile and a Boosey and Hawkes bag.

'Success?' she asked.

'Success!' He looked from her to Lyle Fenton and back again. 'And you?' he asked.

'It was a very good *pasta alla Norma*,' she said.

She stood up, and though shaking hands wasn't a normal thing in her life, it felt like the right thing now. It felt final.

'Thank you for lunch,' she said, as she held out her hand. 'And thank you for meeting me. That's done now, isn't it?'

And she walked out.

She and Ben walked to the underground in silence for a while, and then she said, 'What was Mum thinking, Ben?'

'I'm not sure that thinking came into it,' he said.

And she laughed.

THREE
NOVEMBER

Rula watched her mother haul an enormous pot of goulash out of the oven and set it on a trivet. As she took the lid off and released a heady aroma of meat and vegetables, she said, with her back to Rula, 'I forgot to say, your *ciotka* Julia is coming for lunch today.'

'Why, Mama? She doesn't usually—'

'She's your *babcia's* sister. She can't have Sunday lunch with us?'

'But why today? When—'

'When we finally get to meet your friend. This is exactly why.'

'I don't want to overwhelm her, Mama. There are enough of us already.'

'She's a police inspector, Rula. How she can be overwhelmed by an old lady?' She sprinkled paprika into the pot, and stirred. 'Mind you,' she said, 'she doesn't hear so good these days. I worry she may think your friend is called *Paul*.'

'Mama! Then she'll—'

'Still,' her mother went on, stirring in the paprika, 'she doesn't see so good either, so maybe she won't notice.'

Rula took a spoon out of a drawer, and came to stand by her mother, putting an arm round her waist as she dipped the spoon into the pot and tasted. 'How about you, Mama? Do you wish she was Paul?'

Her mother slapped her hand away, as she was about to dip the spoon in for a second time, and carried the goulash pot back to the oven. 'I wish you can be happy, *kochanie*. If she's good for you, I'll love her. If she's bad for you, I'll kill her.'

'Are we having *pierogi* with the goulash?' Rula asked.

'Of course.'

'Then you are the best mother in the world,' she said.

FOUR
DECEMBER

Picture the scene: a family gathered round a Christmas lunch table, but one far removed from the spacious elegance and polished mahogany that constitute the Platonic ideal of such a table and such a gathering. The room is too small for the table, the table is too small for its occupants, and the people are not quite right, either.

At first sight, they look all right. There is an older couple, nearing sixty, a younger couple, in their thirties, a teenage girl, and three boys, ranging in age, one would say, between nine and thirteen. Grandparents, parents, children. The three boys are quite a brood for the younger couple, but not impossible. So far, so conventional, you would say. But you would be wrong. For a start, the older couple are not married, and though the woman is nearly sixty, the man is not. He is still in his early fifties, but he has had a period of ill-health, which has aged him, and if you are paying attention, you will notice that his seat at the table is a wheelchair. Then, although the older woman is the mother of the younger woman, the older man is not her father, and though the younger couple are married to one another, the teenage girl is the woman's daughter, but not the man's. Of the boys, the middle one is the child of the younger couple (he is dark like his father – you can see the resemblance), the couple are not the parents of the two blond boys. You might think you see a resemblance between them and the younger woman, but that is because they are her brothers – well, half-brothers, actually.

Those of you who have taken an interest in my family will recognise the *dramatis personae* here, of course, and there is really nothing unusual about us. The assumption of the neat, nuclear family is as far from reality as the style magazines' ideal Christmas table is from mine.

So, you see that David is still with us. I apologise for leaving you in the dark about that, but when I walked into that room in the ICU, I really wasn't sure what I was seeing: so many tubes and wires and flashing lights, and David so white and still and bandaged on the bed. I didn't know what to do, but I was urged to squeeze his hand, and, after breathless seconds, he squeezed back.

And so it began, the recovery. No smooth ascent into sunlit uplands, but the bumpiest of journeys: false starts, doubling back, brick walls and treacherous swamps, alongside fury, frustration and despair.

A soon as I could, I confessed my fifteen-year-old crime in not telling him the truth about Ekrem Yilmaz's death. He was less outraged than I expected. He always had his doubts, he said, but he suspected the quiet little Japanese girl who had been on duty in the library the night Yilmaz was crushed by a rolling book stack. So my big reveal was a bit of a non-event, and I feel that I cheated by saving it for a time when David had more urgent things to think about.

But here we are, anyway. Yes, David is still using a wheelchair, but he has rebuffed my offer to cut up his turkey for him today, and he is chatting comfortably with Freda, who is sitting next to him. He is himself, and he is here.

Ellie, Ben and Nico are here too, of course. And the other two boys? Arthur and Hubert, the sons of my ex-husband's widow, the not-so-fragrant-these-days Lavender. Of course it is hard to be left a young widow and single mother in your thirties, but Lavender's approach to the problem has been startling. She immediately found herself a younger lover, and the two of them have embarked on a programme of exotic travel, undertaken whenever they can get away from the up-market riding school which they run in the grounds of her almost-stately home. What the boys get is an expensive public school education, and not much else. They were little monsters when they were young, but boarding school has made them closed and quiet. This has exacerbated Ellie's mother-hen tendencies. Not content with hovering anxiously over her own children, and lavishing pastoral support on her pupils at school, she has taken her brothers into her heart, sending them cakes, visiting on parents' days and sports days, when Lavender is otherwise occupied, and having them to stay for weeks at a time during school holidays. At present, she and Jago (yes, really!) are finding three weeks of winter sun in the Maldives (as Lavender says, *Such a pity that we can only get away during school holidays),* so the boys are here, and next week they will go with Ellie's family to see Ben's parents in Italy, where Epiphany is the big festival. Ben has already honed his step-parenting skills with Freda, and I am watching him now, as he jokes with Arthur and slides one of his pigs-in-blankets onto Hubert's plate. And when they get to Italy, Ben's mother is guaranteed to take them to her ample bosom.

So there we are, and while everyone is happy, and no-one needs me, I am free to contemplate two startling pieces of news. Appropriately for the time of year, both items arrived by post – one of them, indeed, delivered by a postwoman in a Santa hat. The most recent was shown to me by Freda, when she arrived this morning, and I have been so occupied by an oven full of bird, and the juggling of all its accoutrements, that it is only now that I have the brain space to consider its implications. It is a Christmas card, sent from the US, carrying a pen and ink sketch of Virgin and Child, and printed on behalf of the Hospices of the Sisters of Mercy in Boston, Massachusetts. I was mystified until I read the signature, *With love from Faith.* And then I read Faith's message:

Dear Freda, High School in Boston didn't
work out. I just felt too old for it, I guess.
So I am living and working with the Sisters,
and I am very happy. It is what God means
me to do.

What do I feel? Well, this is restorative justice of a quite appropriate kind, isn't it? And I'm in favour of that. On the whole, I think this is as good an outcome as any – it is hard to see the point of her spending her youth in prison. And I can see that it has made Freda feel better. I am bothered by God's involvement, though. I just hope that she doesn't decide at some point that God wants her to put people out of their pain, but I am trusting the good Sisters to have an eye out for that.

The second piece of mail arrived last week, and came addressed jointly to David and to me, which is comparatively rare. It was an invitation:

Paula and Rula
Invite you to join them at their
Civil Partnership Ceremony
In Marlbury Town Hall
On 14th February 2023
At 11.30 am
Lunch afterwards at
The Wagon Wheel,
Lower Shepton
RSVP Rula or Paula
Bartoszrula@gmail.com
PPowell@hotmail.com

Why didn't I see it, I, who pride myself on my sharp perception and acute reading of the human psyche? I couldn't have expected to make an item of Rula and Paula – I've never seen them together – but how was I convinced for years that Paula had a thing for David, and that was why she hated me? It's a worrying question, really, because she did/does hate me, and what other reason could she possibly have?

Anyway, the invitation perked David up no end, and he is fired with a new determination to walk into the ceremony. Actually, he can walk a few steps now, but his balance is still shaky. Finding out what the stumbling blocks – literally – might be for him at the Town Hall, or at the lunch, gave me an excuse to ring Rula, rather than answering by email, and ask nosey questions.

We dealt with *How is David?* and the practicalities quite quickly: no steps into the Town Hall; disabled entrance at the back of the Wagon Wheel if needed. Then I asked about life and work plans.

'I've left the Met,' she told me. 'I've joined the Kent force, and we've bought a cottage near Marlbury.'

'Country life,' I said. 'That's quite a change from Croydon.'

'Well, I'm learning that it isn't all *Garden of England* in East Kent. Paula entrapped me with cosy country pubs, but now I'm seeing the reality.'

'Thanet?' I said.

'All those sad bits of seaside that nobody wants anymore – Margate, Ramsgate, Westgate...' She reeled them off.

'Broadstairs has a certain faded charm,' I said.

'I haven't been sent there yet, so I suppose the crime level is low.'

'Very elderly,' I said.

'But Dover,' she said.

'Poor old Dover, besieged by boats. And then there's the Isle of Sheppey,' I said. 'Devil Island.'

'I haven't been there. When I ask about it my colleagues just roll their eyes. What's wrong with it?'

'I've never been there either, but those who know it tend to mention *inbreeding* in a meaningful tone.'

237

'Couldn't be further away from the London melting pot,' she said. 'Where has Paula brought me?'

'Can I ask you a rather personal question?' I said, getting to the nub of what I really wanted to talk about.

'What?' she asked, definitely on the defensive.

'Why the civil partnership and not marriage?'

'Oh, that's easy.' I heard the relief in her voice. 'I don't want to be a wife – and I don't want to have a wife. *Wife* is someone lesser – it's always *husband and wife*, isn't it – never the other way round – Adam's rib and all that?'

'You weren't ready to *dwindle into a wife.*'

'Dwindle is a good word.'

'It's not original. It's from a play. The heroine states her conditions for marrying her lover, and says that if he accepts them all, then she *"might by degrees dwindle into a wife"*. The play is called *The Way of the World*, and the remarkable thing about it is that it was written in 1700 – and by a man.'

She laughed. 'Well, Paula and I are partners – that's what we are – and the civil partnership suits us very well.'

I didn't ask about her – presumably Catholic – Polish parents, and how they feel. I had probed enough, so I said we were looking forward to the day, and rang off. And I have been thinking about this conversation ever since.

It was nine years ago that David suggested that we got married. It wasn't a romantic proposal: I was going through a bit of a life crisis – both work and family – and he presented me with the option of leaving Marlbury and starting a new life with him in London. I turned him down for reasons which seemed good to me then – mainly that I am six years older than him, and he still had the chance of a proper family life, with children, rather than tying himself to a menopausal old bat. Now, that argument doesn't work so well. David has been aged by his near-death experience, and he needs me. I feel a *Jane Eyre* moment coming on: our independent

heroine can marry her lover only when he is damaged and in need of her. Well, I think my real reason for not marrying David was that, like Rula, I don't want to be a wife. I tried it once, and I was no good at it. And David won't ask me again, anyway. Anything we do will be up to me. In recent weeks, with everything that we have gone through, I have got used to referring to David as *my partner*, when dealing with officialdom, and it is beginning to feel more plausible than it did when we led separate lives. So I will go to Rula's and Paula's party, and see what I think.

Reader, I won't marry him, but I'm in favour of any occasion that involves cake.